The Cathedral

If Bitcoin didn't exist, AI would have invented it.
Brian Roemmele

1. Geon is a pigeon who has taken up residence (with his mate) in our back garden.

Copyright © 2024 Bill Aronson – all rights reserved.

Thank you! A book's author is just the project manager. So many people have contributed to my understanding. This book synthesises the insights of many Bitcoiners. There's not the space to acknowledge you all, but you know who you are.

I want to thank the large and growing team at Bitcoin Policy network, including in alphabetical order: Ashley, Bastien, Clara, Cristina L, Cristina M, Dan, Daniel, Eddie, Freddie, Gareth, Huxley, Ian F, Ian G, Jade, Jennifer, Jeremy Ca, Jeremy Cl, Jordan, Juni, Mark, Matt, Maya, Nick, Nicolas, Richard, Robin, Russell, Sam, Scott, Shreyan, and Susie.

Thank you to Catherine and Zoe, who read the first drafts and encouraged me to continue. Matt, Neil, Patrick, and Will deserve credit for their excellent proofreading and suggestions.

This book is dedicated to Jayesh, the best friend anyone could have. He was fearless.

1: Sam 5

2: Ricky 21

3: Now what? 33

4: Hal 49

5: Money 55

6: Father Christmas 61

7: Zoe 73

8: The Grill 81

9: The Approach 91

10: Arrival 95

11: Bittersweet 107

12: Unexpected Guests 119

13: Home Again 129

14: The Road Back 141

15: To Cambridge 153

16: The Abyss 165

17: The Return 175

18: Notes Part 1: Money & Botcoin 185

19: Notes Part 2: About Hashing 197

20: Description of Botcoin – Draft 205

21: Afterword – Proof of Thought 215

A love note from Hal 225

Suggested Next Steps 229

About the Author 231

1: Sam

It started with a low roar, not animalistic, more mechanical. Then it got louder and louder, its pitch increasing, until the sound was deafening and shrill. There was such urgency, a scream that demanded attention. I touched the control panel, and immediately the cry deflated and was replaced with a sad chicken squawking disappointment, and then silence.

I took the retro kettle off the hob and, with clumsy tremored fingers, made myself a cup of tea. I don't feel old, but my body begs to disagree. I no longer walk but shuffle, and not a soft-shoe shuffle, just a stumbly shuffle. The funny thing is that it's not bad. I used to be terrified of getting old, losing strength, vigour, and mental acuity, but I have learned to accept it, the slow coasting down the hill. I tell you that disappearing testosterone is a blessing. You can see people as they are. Who cares if someone is ugly? I'm no oil painting, all wrinkled and blotchy. No, you look in their eyes, listen to the sound of their voice, their gestures, and see beyond the frailty. I love this little bungalow in the country. While I sip my hot sweet English breakfast tea in the dining room, I can look across the lush green triangle to the manor house that is five hundred years old. When I first moved here, there was a telephone pole, but of course, that's gone. The bright red telephone box is still there. When I was young, they turned it into a de-fib station in case of heart attacks. Now, it's a full-body scanner. You can pop in and check if you are dying. No need for me to use it.

Nowadays, I forget names. Sometimes, I awake and run through the letters of the alphabet, searching for a name of an old friend or colleague. It remains tantalisingly out of reach. Sometimes, hours later, a circuit clicks in my brain, and I remember. But not always. So, there's some urgency. I think it's important you know what really happened.

When I was young, there was a show on TV called *Brain of Britain*, another one called *University Challenge*, and even one called *Who Wants to be a Millionaire?* That would buy you a cup of coffee today, but it was worth something then. The rules were different, but the winner had the best memory. Memory is great, don't get me wrong. But memory is not insight, or understanding, or intelligence. So, here's the secret that my younger self didn't know. It's not that important, more of a nice to have. Who used to say that they had had an apostrophe when they meant they had had an epiphany? It's on the tip of my tongue. There's a Z in there somewhere.

Zoe, her name was Zoe. Yes! I sat down to write. Today is a good day. My mind is clear. I want to record what I can remember, while I still can remember.

I was born on Sunday the 1st October 1989 at Epsom Hospital, Surrey, England, the only son of Thomas and Elizabeth Newman. My father was the town pharmacist and my mother helped him behind the counter and volunteered in the local Oxfam charity shop.

Dad was a small man with a pot belly, a pipe, and an infectious laugh. He went bald in his early twenties. You don't realise that your parent is small when you are a kid, that is until you discover one day that you aren't looking up at him, but looking at him, eye to eye, and then with a snap of a finger and a blur of walks, packed lunches, games, sleeps, and school, now you are looking down on him. I could feel his heart, his warmth, his willingness to help, his kindness, and his secrecy. He spoke quietly, softly, and with a certain assurance but no boldness. He was happiest in the vegetable garden he had made, planting carrots, onions, potatoes, and lettuce – sensible things, as well as a splash of strawberry which would hide under their leaves in case the birds found them, which, of course, they always did.

My mum was tall, thin, underappreciated, privately frustrated at being a mother. She wanted challenge, command, leadership, not laundry and dishes. There was a faraway look in her eye as if she was seeing where she should be, which wasn't as a foundation and support to her husband and child. She dressed impeccably, spoke like royalty in slow measured tones as if she was opening Parliament rather than a tin of beans. She went to the hairdresser once a week not to gossip with the other mothers but to ensure that her black hair was perfect.

My memories of my mum have been reworked so many times that they feel like old photographs. The colours have faded and blued like adverts in the window of a shop that has gone bankrupt. They're no longer real, if they ever were, more like the fragments of a dream half-remembered. What is the difference between memory and imagination? Memory is of the past. Imagination is of the future. But can the mind tell the difference? Perhaps imagination is a memory of the future, and memory just an imaginary past.

One memory, though, is vivid. I must've been about seven. I lay in bed with a fever. I remember the wallpaper was speckled with woodchips. It comforted me to scratch the chips off with my fingernail, making a smooth patch next to my bed. Though I was sick, for some reason, my parents had still gone out for the evening to the theatre. On their return, my mum had come to my room, still dressed in a regal purple velvet gown. I remember the swishing sound that it made and the scent of her perfume. In my fevered state, it was as if the queen had arrived.

She sat on my bed and applied a damp cloth to my brow. The cool was delicious. As she applied the cloth, she sang the French round, *Frères Jacques, Frère Jacques, dormez vous, dormez vous*? I remember this moment so distinctly because ordinarily, she found it hard to express simple mum love. She even hated me calling her Mum. "*So common*", she'd exclaim. For this moment, though, she was loving. I wanted to bathe in her warmth, but it enveloped me, and I felt the release of the drug-like sleep working its way through my body. "*Sing it again*", I said vaguely. Must stay awake. She stroked my burning head. I fell asleep.

I don't know why she found touch so difficult. It wasn't just her relationship with me. She was also chilly with my dad. It wasn't that she didn't love either of us. She just couldn't express it easily.

As a leader in waiting she held her body erect, contained, as if she was about to be announced on stage to give a speech, and needed to rehearse and concentrate on the key points she wanted to get across. You couldn't just jump in her arms. You might muss her hair or get dirt on her immaculate dress.

I remember one Sunday when we all went in the car to the Thames near Kew Gardens. I must've been around seven or eight. I'm not sure. They walked leisurely along the side of the river while I ran ahead. I was in my fantasy world, an explorer fighting off pirates. I found a stick and was slashing at the long grass, forcing invisible enemies to the ground, offering no mercy.

Soon, I was out of sight. When I eventually doubled back to rejoin them, I turned the corner to see something I found shocking and horrifying. My mother and father were locked in a warm embrace. There was nobody else around. For a moment, this incongruous couple, my father short and stout, my mother towering over him, were holding each other so tenderly, I almost tripped and fell over.

The stick fell forgotten from my hand.

It was the last time I saw them so affectionate with each other. In that moment, I felt like an intruder, an outsider. My father saw me out of the corner of his eye, and the moment was gone.

Later that year, I sensed a change in the household. There were important meetings that they went to. *"No darling, you can't come. You would be bored anyway. Just grown-up stuff. Who do you want to go and play with? We will be back in a few hours."*

Then I found pills in her bedside drawer. Lots of pills with different names that I couldn't pronounce. Two to be taken three times a day. Take after a meal. Do not take on an empty stomach. Take on an empty stomach. She had always been slim, but now she was gaunt and often pressed her hand on her lower back and winced. She took to wearing a turban. *"What do you think? Very fashionable. I think it's all the rage."* My father agreed and bit his lip. Then we got a cleaner and a cook. I peeped into her bedroom once and saw her without her turban. She had no hair.

Not long after, she died of complications from breast cancer. I wasn't there when it happened. I'd been sent away to my father's sister's house in Oxfordshire. When I came back, she was gone. They'd decided that I shouldn't attend her funeral because it would be too distressing. I was eight. I should have been there.

Geon looked at me. He had the good sense not to say *literally*. There were tears in my eyes. Such a long, long time ago. What a terrible decision, to prevent me from knowing that she'd died, to experience her gone, to see her still, unmoving, to sing the funeral songs, feel the icy coldness of her hand, and throw dirt in the grave. It made me numb. Literally. I mustn't dwell on it, though. When I do it makes me burn with anger. The injustice. Take a deep breath.

This isn't an autobiography. I just want you to understand a few things about me so that you realise it wasn't really accidental that I ended up in the story. I'm not saying I was special. I'm sure there could have been hundreds of other people who could have played the same role, but if they had, then they would have had similar experiences that made them – let's be honest and say it – unemotional loners. Moving right along. Three years go by.

Wait, I can't leave out my dog and cat. The dog was a sociable, playful cocker spaniel called Ginny. The cat never got a name and was just Cat. Ginny was focused on fun. She wasn't introspective. When dogs want to complete a conversation and change the subject, they shake themselves in the same way as they do when they emerge from a swim in the sea. Shake. Shake. Shake. That's done. What's next?

Cat was striped vaguely like a tiger, moved slowly and carefully, and treated us with disdain. He lived outside and only came in to eat and sleep at night, curled up on the living room sofa, never on my bed.

Ginny and I were playing in my bedroom once when she suddenly saw herself in the mirror. Her hair stood up, and I could see the look of shock on her face. She looked at me quizzically. *What's that? Is that another dog? Is that me?* This moment was earth-shattering for Ginny. What would she do?

Shake. Shake. Shake. Let's go play. After that, I would sometimes bring her to the mirror and point, but there was never any flicker of recognition. A year later, when Cat decided it was time to die, he was very matter-of-fact. First, he dug himself a shallow grave amongst the potatoes and then circled the house three times, yowling at the top of his voice to let everyone know that something important was about to happen.

Then he lay down in the grave and was still. That was it. Ginny was devastated. So that Cat would not be forgotten he took on his personality. Ginny became aloof, standoffish, and now insisted on sleeping on the sofa instead of her basket in the kitchen, and spending much of the day outside. Good on you Ginny.

When I was eleven, my father had me take a Mensa IQ test. I'm not sure why. Mensa was the snobby society for the super-intelligent. An average IQ is 100. To join Mensa, you need an IQ of 130 which is higher than 98% of the population. Einstein never did an IQ test, but his was estimated at 160.

I didn't prepare. I couldn't see the point, which made my dad irritated. If you plot a large group of people, their IQs form a bell curve. The typical bell curve only displays three standard deviations at 115, 130, and 145. My score came back at 178, or five standard deviations – literally off the chart. My dad didn't believe it and rang up to complain. They agreed that I could redo the test at no charge. This time, I scored 179.

The mistake wasn't the score. The mistake was believing that the IQ test had any meaning. We were both gullible. I knew nothing of the other kinds of intelligence – emotional, streetwise, body, to name a few.

My character has always been rational, logical, some even say autistic. I don't see the point of small talk. It's so boring. Can we just get on and talk about the important stuff? Facts matter. Ideas matter. Feelings don't. I write in short sentences with no room for emotional foliage.

I didn't understand that small talk was like massage oil, rubbing away the frictions and knots in relationships and setting the scene for greater trust and intimacy. I've got better over time, but I still find relationships exhausting, baffling, and depleting. Literally.

Being labelled a genius is a disability. You think you're smarter than everyone else because there would probably not be more than five hundred people in the world or five in Great Britain with a similar score. That makes you arrogant and others resentful. It would take me many years to realise that a high IQ just means you see the world in a different light, nothing more or less. It would take me even longer to realise the test was bullshit. None of the people who developed or popularised it ever bothered to take the test themselves, or if they did, they kept the result private. One thing was certain. Nobody with a high IQ would have created such a test.

On Sunday, September 9th, 2001, just before my twelfth birthday, my life changed again. Instead of attending the local grammar school, my father sent me to Deerborne, a second-tier private school in Wiltshire. In England for some reason due to the quirk of the English psyche, *private* schools are called *public* schools. Deerborne was a wannabe Winchester, Harrow, or Eton. It even had the same style of architecture, quadrangles, coats of arms, lavish use of sandstone – but it was all fake, created in the 1950s, just after the war.

I hated it. For years after I left, I couldn't describe my experiences there without ending up quivering with anger within a few minutes. I didn't understand why my dad sent me there, this fake, stuffy, manicured hellhole. I was desperately lonely and homesick. I felt I must have done something wrong, but what, I didn't know.

Deerborne was an all-boys boarding school. To me, some of the customs were arcane and baffling. The school song was in Latin to make it seem ancient and classy. The boys wore starched collars as if they were Edwardians. There were three offences that could get you suspended or expelled – eating fish and chips, going to the local cinema, or meeting girls. Anyone who could achieve the trifecta and not get caught, eat fish and chips in a movie, with their arm around a girl, gained mythic status. I never did.

All first-year students lived in Elmwood House. I remember my father helping me bring my trunk in.

I'm panicking. My starched collar chafes and burns my neck. My tie is crooked and twisted. I still haven't got the hang of it despite several hours coaching with my father in front of the mirror. My boater, the scratchy straw hat we have to wear, is rigid and inflexible. I'm hot, sweaty, and terrified.

Mr Grey, the housemaster, is standing in the shadow at the front door, greeting parents and students. He's very tall and very round. He reminds me of Humpty Dumpty. He speaks in a loud, booming voice. Everything about Mr Grey is large. Large nose, large ears, large bum, large feet. We say hello, go upstairs and dump my belongings on my bed. My father leaves abruptly. I'm close to tears. How am I going to survive this? Maybe it's good that I can numb myself. If I shut down, perhaps I'll be OK. I start counting. Forty-five days to the mid-term break. One hundred days to end of term. Stay numb. Survive.

The next morning, the prefects wake us up at 5 am and march us down to the basement where Mr Grey is waiting by the side of a plunge pool, dressed only in a white bathrobe like he'd just wandered in from a five-star spa. Yesterday with the parents, he was delightful, polite, considerate, and charming, but this morning he's hard, cold, and indifferent.

"Clothes OFF! Form up in rows of four or five!" he barked.

He blew sharply on a whistle which hung on a string from his neck. The echo reverberated around the room.

There was a pause; then, reluctantly, we did what we were told. The prefects stood to one side, smirking.

I was in the first row of naked, squirming boys, their hands twisted with shame in front of their tiny dicks.

Mr Grey blew his whistle again.

"Jump in!" he commanded.

We jumped. The shock of the frozen water burst across my body. I accidentally gulped some water and swam, choking to the other side. One of the prefects pulled me out, and I lay on the cold tiles like a fish, coughing and spitting.

"Get up that boy! Stop wasting time!" Mr Grey said sarcastically.

I didn't have a name, not even a number. I was just "that boy", one of many. I smelt the chlorine and felt the dank, cold, slightly mouldy roughness of the tiles. My elbows were scraped and had thin beads of blood from the scratches by being roughly rescued.

I pushed myself up onto my knees, and then stood up, grabbing a thin towel to make myself less vulnerable. dry myself off.

The process repeated. In the last row, one boy couldn't swim, so had to be pulled out of the water before he drowned. Nobody had thought to ask him. He writhed and squealed before the prefects got him out and then cried – something that I knew instinctively you must never do.

After three days of this torture, I decided to act. In a break from school, I cycled into town, and found a hardware store that sold powdered paint. I bought a big pot of yellow dye and emptied it into the water. The next morning the water was tinted and perhaps tainted, so our ablutions were cancelled. It took them the whole of the next day to scrub the pool out. I continued my terrorist campaign.

One day, I found a dead rat on the side of the bike path near the playing fields. I was delighted and gingerly manoeuvred it into a plastic shopping bag without touching it. It would be perfect. When we came down the next morning, we saw its mouth contorted in a grimace as it floated in the middle of the pool, looking like a self-satisfied smile. *"Sir! Sir, there's a dead rat in the pool. We can't swim in that!"* Another day, I got a large saucepan of stew from the kitchen. *"Sir! Looks like someone's been sick in the pool."* Mr Grey's fury was barely contained. It was time to take it up a notch. It was time for the coup de grâce. The next morning the boys arrived to see Mr Grey trying to use a net to fish out my shit which was bobbing gayly and merrily in the centre of the pool. He overreached and slipped into the water. Blindly pushing the shit away, he didn't realise that one little fellah was on the top of his head. This was too much. Everyone burst into laughter, followed by a moment of pin-drop silence into which one boy whispered, *"Sir, that's disgusting."* It was like a scene from Lord of the Flies.

We discovered something about Mr Grey that morning, something that he'd been at pains to keep secret. It was something that he was ashamed of because it didn't fit with his carefully manicured image of himself. He couldn't swim. I'll never forget the sound he made. He squealed like a pig, his eyes wide with terror. Then he took another swig of shitty water, which abruptly silenced him, his arm twirled like he was waving goodbye, and then he sank like a stone. It didn't seem possible that someone so big wouldn't float. But he didn't.

For a moment, nobody moved. Then the two prefects argued about who should rescue him because nobody wanted to get in *that* water, and besides, he was as big as a walrus. While they bickered, Mr Grey patiently lay inert on the bottom and died.

I burned inside with icy cold terror. I was paralysed by fear. My legs felt like jelly. My brain was overloaded with catastrophic expectations. *"There's the culprit. Seize him!"* What ifs flew around my brain like flies caught inside a greenhouse on a summer's day. My heart beat so fast I was sure that everyone must hear it. I had bouts of diarrhoea, and while on the toilet, my ears were attuned to every slightest sound. When were they coming for me? And to think I had only been here a week!

That was the last time we used the plunge pool. After that the morning dips were cancelled by the new housemaster. Nobody ever found out who did it, but the story grew with exaggeration, as it did the rounds of the school. There was even talk that he'd been in hiding and that they, whoever they were, had finally caught up with him. He had been assassinated. As the stories got wilder and wilder, the simple truth that my prank had gone horribly wrong was mercifully forgotten.

I'm so sorry. I forgot to mention my name; I just assumed you knew. Silly me. I forgot to mention that. I just said that. I'm repeating myself. This is my memoir. There's so much guff written about that time; I thought I should give you my side of the story. I'll probably lie, embellish the truth, make stuff up. That's OK. It's a story. Every time I remember something, I change it subtly. I'm not doing that deliberately; it's just my way of making sense of the world now.

I've done it again, gone off on a side track. Should I say my name is Sam, or I'm Sam? I never know which is right. My name is Sam, is more accurate. I'm not Sam. That's just a word, a convenient label. Perhaps I'm overthinking it. I'm Sam, sounds more friendly. I'll go with that. I'm Sam.

2 Ginny and I were playing in my bedroom once when she suddenly saw herself in the mirror.

2: Ricky

I've been meaning to introduce Geon pronounced Jon. Geon is a pigeon who has taken up residence in our back garden. Oh, I already did? Are you sure? OK.

Like me, Geon thinks he owns the place. Do you know what a pigeon looks like? Grey colours and serious-looking beady black eyes. You must have seen films of them. They used to be as common as mice, and there are still some parts of the world where you can find them.

If you don't know what they are, look it up. That sounded a bit tetchy. Sorry. I don't have time to describe them. I say he, but I have no idea of his gender, and it's not something that comes up in our conversation.

He likes to repeat himself. When he's happy and satisfied, I think he says *"literally"* in a soft, breathy way, as you might say, when laying your head down on a soft pillow in a bed with clean sheets. *"Literally"*. There's a slight pause as he contemplates how perfectly it expresses his feelings. And then again, with absolute certainty and conviction, *"literally"*. Pause. "literally". Over and over, it's his mantra. He looks at me. *"What do you think?"* he seems to say. *"I wish I could be as eloquent"*, I reply. And then, at a certain point, he flaps off.

By the time I was fifteen, I'd left Elmwood and had been living for two years in Red House. I'd learned how to survive and was part of a gang of friends.

Phillip was the acknowledged leader. He was strategic, cautious, and knew how to manipulate. He didn't look like how I imagined a leader. His skin was pasty, his forehead covered in blackheads. He peered out from thick glasses. He wasn't particularly tall, nor athletic, not even extroverted. His hair was greasy. Yet somehow, he held sway over us.

George was an open book, physical, ruddy, athletic. His parents lived in Singapore. That seemed very exotic to us.

David was the troubadour, often composing a song on his guitar in a corner, his attempt to alleviate the self-doubts that plagued us all.

Len was the intellectual, always first in the class, with a biting wit that he used to wound or impress.

Phillip's control came from his seething volcanic anger, which strangely didn't affect me, but I could see its effect on others. I was Phillip's lieutenant, and enforcer. We were tight.

Deerborne was a boarding school. Each year slept in their own dormitory with an older prefect maintaining discipline. Phillip and I had been chosen to be dormitory prefects for the two years below. As I was about to turn sixteen, I returned to Deerborne to find that I was next door in charge of the fourteen-year-olds while Phillip oversaw the year above. And that's when the trouble came.

Our beds were allocated, and I found myself in the last bed. Next to me was Ricky. I'd been obsessed with Ricky for months. Ricky was the most beautiful boy I had ever seen in my life. He was lithe, feminine, softly spoken, and graceful. I couldn't keep my eyes off him. And now I was in the bed next to his.

I willed myself to sleep for the first few nights back at school. Then, there was a full moon and a cloudless sky. I absorbed the moon, so perfect and out of reach. I gradually reached out across the expanse that separated the beds, moving slowly in case anyone else was awake. My heart was pounding. My throat was dry. I heard the sound of bed springs from the other side of the room and withdrew instantly. I knew the punishment if I was caught. Since Mr Grey's death, I'd learned all about secrecy. It was my constant companion.

The next night, I tried again. This time, imperceptibly, I made it to the other shore and felt the rough texture of the school blankets. Inch by inch, I found a way in and felt the warmth of his body just inches from my fingertips—soft fire. I touched the skin of his belly. This was the moment of truth. If he rejected me, I would be destroyed. Instead, he took my hand and guided me down. The secret silence. The quickened breath.

Over the next few nights, we gradually explored each other. I would come into his bed in the middle of the night while others slept. We were coming closer, more intimate, enjoying each other. But at the same time, I felt a deep and growing shame. How could I destroy Ricky's innocence? My guilt grew until I could stand it no longer.

I went to see Phillip and asked him if we could swap dormitories. He looked at me quizzically. *"Why?"* he asked bluntly. Eventually, my face burning, and with promises of absolute secrecy, I told him, though I knew I was betraying myself and putting myself in a precarious position. I was impulsive. I just wanted the feeling of guilt and shame to go away. I saw him contemplating and calculating. Then he agreed to make the switch, and I met Ricky and told him it was over. I could tell he was disappointed and simultaneously conflicted.

It didn't occur to me that he was also falling for me. I was in a blind panic, blundering my way forward, desperate to survive.

A week later, I noticed everyone looking at me as I entered the common room. I didn't realise it then, but I can feel energy. It's an ability that has been with me forever, so it just feels natural and normal. Doesn't everyone? Maybe not. At the time, I would probably have said I could feel their eyes on me without realising that logically makes no sense. How can eyes and skin be so connected? There's a quite different feeling on my skin if I'm the centre of attention. There was an icy silence. Some of my friends avoided my gaze. Others stared with micro-smiles. They knew. Phillip had told everyone. It was a social death.

I'm sitting in my favourite chair in the living room. From where I sit, I can see a grey horse and a young girl rider trot by on the lane in front of the triangular green. There is no more beautiful sound than the clop, clop, clop of hooves on tarmac. I can hear Geon talking to himself on the back deck, looking for seeds the smaller birds have discarded from the bird feeder. Where was I? Oh yes, Phillip. It turned out that as soon as he had switched beds with me, he started an affair with Ricky himself on the very same day that he'd started a whispering campaign about me.

It wasn't uncommon; what do you expect when you cram hundreds of boy teenagers into isolation? Hypocrisy, passion, jealousy, and sex all colliding with each other.

I spent the next two years isolated and alone. I was part of no peer group. I buried my head in my studies and went for long walks in the nearby Deerborne Castle estate. Looking back, I can see that this time shaped me. I wouldn't say I was grateful, but it meant that I could concentrate for long periods and go deeper and deeper into anything I was curious about, like a diver who pushes down determined to get to the seabed, even though their lungs are screaming, whatever the cost. I began to see that complexity, which initially seems baffling and impossible to understand, is just an awful lot of simplicity. At first, problems seem ginormous, and I feel stupid and dull. Then a pattern emerges, and another, and another, and the problem shrinks until I am looking down on it, as small as a rabbit.

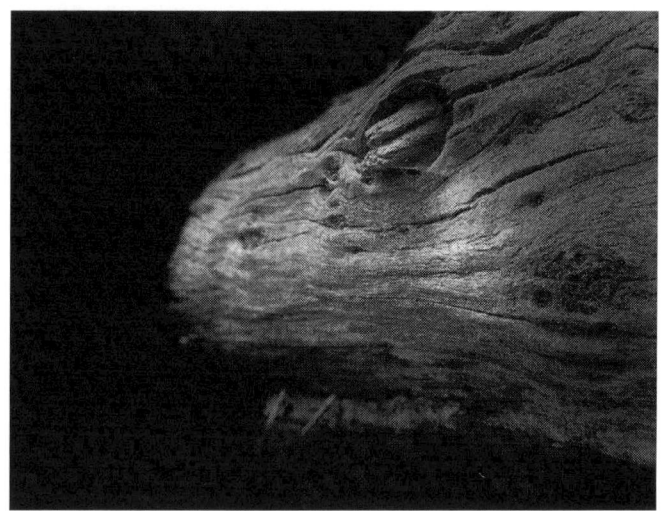

3 Dragon Tree

I took my camera. One day, I noticed that the whorls of a tree trunk looked like a person's face. It became a fascination. I found crocodiles, elephants, and bears. Some were strange, melted, and distorted. I curated the best photos and stored them in a folder on my computer. Perhaps one day, I would share them.

Although I was a pariah, there was one area of my school life which seemed to be exempt. Rugby or Rugger, as we called it. In the classroom, I sat alone, clenching my arse, all the while feeling tormented by thoughts and willing time to move faster. In the dormitory, nobody wanted to be in the bed next to me. But on the rugby pitch, I had a special skill and a natural talent. It was if the rugby pitch was another dimension where the normal rules of ostracisation didn't apply, and outright war could be played out. If I had seen a therapist at the time, they would have said I was depressed. Take a complex set of feelings, sensations, memories, and emotions and throw a single-word blanket over them. If I could've articulated what I felt at the time, which I wouldn't and couldn't, I would probably have just said that's just life, its normal.

In the heart of the rugby scrum, the hooker's role is to hook the ball back. The timing was everything. Move too fast, and the other team will get a penalty. Too slow, and they would tuck the ball back into the safety of the back of their scrum, taunting the opposing scrumhalf to move too fast.

This was my skill – to hook. When the two teams hunkered down, the pressure on the front row was enormous. Sometimes, my arms felt like they were being pulled out of their sockets. At other times, I could be lifted into the air.

My timing was almost always perfect, and each time I tapped the ball back, I felt my opponent become more frustrated and pressured by their team's disappointment. Sometimes, realising that they couldn't win the ball, they would deliberately kick my shins. It wasn't uncommon for me to walk off the pitch at the end of the game with blood trickling through my socks. I didn't care. I was accepted. I was trusted.

I turned eighteen in October 2007. Because of my ability, I was selected to be in the first fifteen. Our team played across England, competing against schools far more prestigious than ours. Often, my ability in the scrum tilted the scales in our favour. I felt proud, energised, and strong when I walked onto the rugby field. This was where I was at my best. Free of Deerborne's suppressing confines, I felt an unstoppable passion and belonging; I was a driving force on the field, a star, a hero, a god. Well, maybe that's going a bit far, but you know what I mean.

I remember the date. 5th April 2008. It was the penultimate game of the season, and we were at home playing Winchester, one of the best teams in the competition. The Winchester hooker knew of my reputation but was confident that he could beat me. Who had ever heard of Deerborne? He didn't know I had nothing to lose. This was the only time when I was trusted and accepted and when I could truly fly. In that game, I dominated the scrums, and even though they were a better team, we held them to 12 all. At half-time, I saw their captain having a word with his teammates and glancing in my direction. There was no way that Winchester would lose to a tinpot school like ours.

Somehow, we managed to hold them off. The score remained even throughout the second half. With five minutes left on the clock, another scrum was called within twenty yards of their line. The two rucks crunched together, and immediately, Winchester wheeled the scrum so that, for a moment, the referee couldn't see what was about to happen. I felt a sickening crunch in my right leg. There was no pain, just astonishment. Instinctively, I knew what had happened. I heard my opponent give an involuntary giggle. I looked down, and my leg was at an impossible angle. The scrum caved and collapsed, and I pillowed the soft mud on my cheek. I heard the whistle and then nothing. Blackness.

When I awoke, I was in the school hospital. My father was at the end of my bed, looking concerned. My right leg was in plaster and elevated in a harness. I felt a dull pain and throbbing in my shin. My throat was rasping from where they'd forced a breathing tube in as I was under general anaesthetic. In fact, my throat hurt more than my leg. I felt groggy, disorientated, and confused. Then I remembered.

"*Did we win?*" I croaked. My father chuckled wryly.

The school had called him and because it was a day off, he could jump into his car and come straight down. He didn't feel that he needed to do anything. He knew the hospital staff would have everything under control, but he wanted to be there in time for when I came around. He arrived while I was in recovery and spoke to the surgeon, who briefed him on the injury and the plate and pins they had used. The surgeon was relaxed. "*There were no complications. We'll keep him in for a couple of days, but at that age, he'll heal quickly. He'll need to do some physio, but I'm not expecting any problems. You can go in and wait till he wakes up. His leg will hurt. If it gets too bad, we can give him some morphine to manage the pain.*"

"Yes. He was sent off, and your team was awarded a penalty kick at goal. You won 15-12. Everyone says you were a hero." I could feel his love and pride.

There was a silence as I slowly processed what he was saying. I was having difficulty concentrating.

"How long will I be in bed? We still have one more game." I paused. *"When can I go back to training?"* My father hesitated. *"Let's not talk about that right now. Just get some rest."* I drifted off.

4 Swan Tree

5 Happy Tree

3: Now what?

Since I turned seventy, often when I awake, a poem has been fully formed in my head. Today was such a day. I took a sip of water and wrote it down.

Let us lie upon the ledge / the brisk moon moving along / makes pale the cliff that has been our constant companion. / These past weeks / I whisper stories of another place / another world / in your exhausted ear / until your imagination catches fire and brings warmth back into frozen limbs / my voice mingles with the sound of coffee drunk from metal cups / I have captured your eyes / and you move closer / warmth against warmth / life against life, / You say "break that which is brittle within me". / I say "l will not circle round you / but will wait till an emptiness appears / then my heart arrow will quiver past long lost hurt / seeking out that place / beyond childhood grief / beyond desolation / beyond all hope / calling you out to lie beneath the moon / upon a cliff / upon a ledge."

~

I was in the hospital for a week before they allowed me out. Back in January, if my A-level results were good enough, I'd been accepted to Emmanuel College, Cambridge, to study History. The day before my injury, I'd completed my mock exams and knew I'd done well. I was at a loose end with just two months of school remaining. I would have enough time to revise for the exams in June.

My doctor wanted me to use a wheelchair. She explained that it would make my recovery faster and support healing. I refused. I didn't want to be dependent on anyone pushing me around. Who would even agree to do that? She had no idea of my pariah status. I hadn't even told my father. I insisted on using crutches, and she reluctantly agreed.

When I hobbled back into school, it was as if a truce had been reached. People actually clapped when I entered the common room. One person slapped my back so hard that I almost fell over. But my celebrity status wore off within a few days, and I returned to the familiar solitude. Perhaps if it wasn't the end of the last term of the last year at school, I might have made friends if there were more than a couple of months. But it wasn't to be. I didn't mind. I was used to it. It felt normal. I took comfort in knowing that my days at Deerborne were ending.

I remembered a school trip to France. We travelled on the D2009 through the Beauce region and stopped as one of the boys was car-sick. Where we had pulled over was a particularly straight section that extended for approximately 15 miles. I got out to stretch. This road is known for its flatness and long, uninterrupted visibility across the plains. There was no other traffic, and I saw a truck away in the distance, slowly approaching us. For ages, it was far away. Then suddenly, it was thundering towards us, only a hundred yards away, at most. Nobody else had left the bus after me, as an argument had broken out at the back. I could hear chants of "fight, fight, fight", and the driver left his seat to get the situation under control.

I don't know why my gaze was on the truck. Something just felt odd. In slow motion, I saw that the rear axle was telescoping out, and within seconds, the wheel came away and spun towards us. There was nothing to do, nowhere to run. The wheel must have been four feet high. It passed within a whisker between me and the sick boy, who was bent over throwing up and didn't even see it. It crashed into the field of corn behind. I was frozen in silence.

I realised nobody else had seen what had just happened, and nobody would have believed me. Our driver was shouting and frantically trying to restore order on the bus as the boys became increasingly raucous. The truck stopped skidding, and its driver got out shaken. He approached me and asked me in French if I had a cigarette. When I indicated no, he wandered back pale and shaken to his broken truck. With calm restored, our driver called for us to return to the bus, and we drove off.

I remembered that moment from the previous summer and wondered if leaving Deerborne was the same – an event far in the future forever and then suddenly there. I hoped that when it arrived, it wouldn't come accompanied by a metaphorical wheel making a beeline for me.

With limited mobility, I found myself hanging out in the computer science room. There was a smattering of us hunkered and absorbed in the makeshift room;

playing around on the computers was a good distraction. I'd come to terms with the fact that I would never play rugby again, and because I'd ignored my doctor's advice, I might well have a permanent limp.

I discovered a new world. There was a well-worn Visual Basic manual in the computer library, and this became my Bible. Every time I wrote code that worked, I felt a deep satisfaction. Code had a beauty and elegance to it. Pretty soon, I was playing around with Java and PHP, honing my skills, deepening my understanding, and becoming increasingly immersed in the digital world. I enjoyed creating games, and then I started teaching myself C++. There were tons of online resources and chat rooms where I could get help. I felt like I was in a vast computer game, and I'd just jumped up a level with new powers and possibilities. The few others who hung out there were dawning nerds, outcasts like me. We hardly chatted. I'd found a new outlet.

I was annoyed that I'd never shown much interest in computers before. It was partly because I found the computer science teacher, Mr Hurry, creepy. He showed a little too much interest in the students. As he moved around the class, he'd often leave his hands on our shoulders for a long time, which felt unnecessary and disturbing. I always unconsciously tightened the muscles in my arse and back when he approached.

The last day of school was Saturday, June 28th. I remember the date very clearly. I'd finally created a basic flying game using FlightGear, an open-source platform. I was proud of my achievement. Even though I was stuck in the physical world, I could now soar in the clouds in the digital world, as I had done so well on the rugby field.

With some help from one of the school kitchen staff, I packed my bags and trunk one last time and took them downstairs. Things were finally looking up. Everyone was excited to be leaving for the summer. My dad was driving down to pick me up, and I couldn't wait to share my excitement with him. I was sick of school and was impatient to get out of there—free at last.

I sat on the low wall of the quadrangle, bathing in the summer sun. For some reason, there was a strong, sickly-sweet smell of creosote. Everyone was chattering and gossiping. As the minutes ticked away, parents arrived, car boots were popped, dogs barked, instructions were given, and slowly, slowly, the quadrangle emptied.

My carefree excitement was replaced with a mild unease. I called his mobile. No answer. I texted him. No reply. Something was wrong. Annoyance and fear collided in my belly. My father was always reliable. He was never late. I could always count on him. The last student left with their family, and I was alone. The only sounds were the birds and the occasional distant passing car, creating an unbearable emptiness. Where is my father? My only connection beyond Deerborne, and my escape route from these painful years.

Finally, I went to the school office. Everyone had left except the administrator, who was tidying and about to lock up. I explained that my father hadn't come. I noticed that my voice was a little shaky. He must've done as well.

"*My father was supposed to pick me up at 3 pm, and it's now 4:15. He's never late, and I've tried calling and texting, but there's been no response.*"

The administrator, looking concerned, inquired, "*You're Sam Newman, aren't you? Have you tried calling home?*"

"*No,*" I replied, puzzled. "*Why would he be at home, sir? He had texted me when he left to say he was on his way.*"

The administrator suggested, "*Can you try it just to be sure?*"

With a sense of foreboding, I rang home, my heart pounding. After a dozen rings, my father's voicemail greeted me, further deepening my worry. "*No answer from home, sir,*" I reported back.

"*Righto, wait here. I'll go and see what I can find out,*" the administrator instructed. He headed back into his office, where I could just hear him making several phone calls.

I sat in an overstuffed armchair; school was always noisy. Now, my thoughts raced in the eerie silence. The only sounds were those of the old grandfather clock, its steady tick, tick, tick, and occasional wooden clunk, making me increasingly anxious. I watched the clock's hands move slowly until it chimed 5 p.m., marking another hour. I willed my father to walk into the room with an apology and explanation.

Moments later, not my father but the headmaster entered the room and sat down next to me. This was unexpected and unsettling. In my entire time at the school, the headmaster had been a distant figure, a god far away. He didn't even have a name—he was always just *"Headmaster."*

I had only had one conversation with him throughout my school career, and that was two years ago.

My father, the local pharmacist, had often sent me parcels of gifts for my birthday, as it never fell in the holidays. On one occasion, he'd grabbed a large brown box from the pharmacy, which had been used to hold ten smaller brown packs of syringes. He hadn't removed the last two packs from the bottom by mistake. When I opened the present, expecting the usual assortment of socks, chocolates, and a novel, I found the syringe packs stuck to the bottom. It was an easy mistake to make. I dismissed it as another of my father's absentminded moments and stuffed the gifts and the syringes in my locker.

Unfortunately, the housemaster chose to conduct a random locker check the next day while we were in class. When he discovered the syringes, he jumped to conclusions, suspecting me of running a drug ring. Instead of calling me in, he went straight to the headmaster in a frenzy. I was summoned to his office, my knees trembling with anxiety. Nobody ever gets called to the headmaster. What could I have possibly done? On his desk sat the two packs of syringes, a damning sight.

"*What are these?*" he thundered, his voice filled with accusation. He paused between each word for effect.

I nervously mumbled about the mix-up, but he wasn't interested. "*I'm afraid we must send you to see the school doctor, just to be sure. You understand?*" he demanded. No, I didn't. But I'd no choice.

The doctor, though apologetic, performed the necessary examination. "*I'm sorry I must do this, but please roll up your sleeves. I need to check you for track marks*," she said kindly but firmly. I didn't even know what she meant by track marks. Of course, there was nothing to see, nothing to find.

When they realised their mistake, I'd expected them to say sorry—silly me. The headmaster never saw fit to offer an apology. Why should he? I was just a kid. I burned with anger at the injustice. Why had nobody listened to me? Why was I not trusted? Another of Deerborne's finest moments.

Now, we sat in an uncomfortable silence. I could tell he was trying to find the right words, and I wasn't going to help him. He gave a slight cough, swallowed, and ploughed in. "*Look, old chap, I'm sorry to say there was an accident.*"

I said nothing. What could I say? I loathed the man.

"*Yes,*" he continued. I was surprised by how gentle he sounded. "*I'm very sorry to tell you that Mr Newman, your father, appears to have lost control of his car on his way while driving here."*

I was having a tough time grasping what he was saying. Of course, I knew, but I thought if nothing were said, then it wouldn't be real. *"But he's alright, isn't he?"* I answered hopefully. My voice trailed off, my skin prickling as I nosedived into the abyss.

The headmaster again swallowed hard, a painful moment of hesitation. "It seems that his *car went off the road at Padstow Gorge. I'm very, very, very sorry,"* he said as if repeating the word '*very*' several times would make everything clear to me. I could tell that he meant it. He really was sorry. And then, he spoiled it by using the ridiculous words often heard in movies. *"It would have been swift. He wouldn't have felt a thing."* Seriously? No. Even in my shock, his answer sounded rehearsed and contrived.

The silence in the room was only punctuated by the clock. Not knowing what to do, the headmaster seemed to want to offer more comfort. He tried to reach out and hold my hand, but that was too much. I flinched and pulled away.

When I'm upset, I rehearse my replies. Should I say this? Should I say that? I'm afraid to become overwhelmed with emotion. I want to scream and explode; I know it would make me feel great, a huge release, but then afterwards, I would be mortified. I would have embarrassed myself and lost the argument.

Still, it's tempting just to say exactly what I think and not care about the consequences. I practice what to say. I repeat the same arguments in my head, round and round. The anger seethes. I can only react, not respond. If I try a diplomatic phrase, it sounds like a copout. If I try to be authoritative and strident, it sounds squeaky. If I say nothing, I feel paralysed. The only solution is to calm down and wait. But sometimes, there is no time to wait—fight, flight, or freeze. None of them feel good. I can ask a friend or loved one what they think. But then that just drags them into the sorry mess. Take a breath. Wait. Be patient.

The light was fading on the green. Geon had left to sleep wherever that was. I remember spending an extra night at the school while they made phone calls to figure out what to do with me. My aunt came to collect me the next day. She was ten years younger than my father and had just retired from a career in government, working for the Home Office. She took care of me for the next month, arranged the funeral, and otherwise left me alone, except for one occasion. How did I feel? Frankly, I don't remember. I think I was just numb.

I was in my room, on my computer, when my aunt knocked on the door. *"I'm going to the funeral home. I think you should come"*.

This was a moment that I had been dreading. Should I see my father's body? I didn't want to, but I was also morbidly curious. What would he look like? I looked at my aunt. I saw that this wasn't a request but an order.

"Why?"

"It's important," she said without explanation.

We drove to the funeral home in silence. When we arrived, she switched off the ignition and turned to me. *"I will talk with the undertaker while you go in and see him. Logically, we know that he's dead, but our bodies aren't rational. You need to see him to know that it is true. If there is anything you want to say to him, now is your chance."*

The undertaker took me into a small, dimly lit room and then left. It was a shock to see my father lying there in his Sunday best. His face looked different, and his neck was far fatter than I remembered. I hardly recognised him. There was an icy stillness in the room. I didn't want to touch him. I was repelled by his presence. I was afraid that I'd be infected by his death if I touched him. I was tongue-tied. What do you say to someone who can't hear or talk back? I didn't want my aunt or the undertaker to hear my conversation; besides, I was at a loss for what to say. Finally, I whispered in his ear "*goodbye*" and walked quickly out. It seemed so inadequate. I pushed through the swing doors, walked out to the car park, and stood leaning on the car. My aunt followed me out and said nothing.

It was drizzling on the day of the funeral. Walking into the church, I was struck that the pews were full. I'd had nothing to do with the arrangements, so I didn't expect a sea of faces. As I entered, gripping my aunt's arm, I was overwhelmed with grief, compounded by the sad faces that all turned to look at me. I hated being the centre of attention.

My aunt gently guided me to the front pew. My knees were shaking. I sat down and looked at the large portrait of my father in front of an extravagance of flowers.

Within seconds, the organ struck up *"All You Need is Love"* by the Beatles, and surprised laughter peeled through the congregation. My aunt turned to me, smiled, and whispered, "I wanted it to be light and playful. Let's celebrate, and after the service, we can go and get drunk." This was so unexpected; I didn't know whether to laugh or cry.

When the service was over, we stood at the entrance as people approached and offered their condolences. There were some, like Mrs Jenkins, who used to clean the house after my mother died. I'd known her for years. *"I'm so sorry, Sam. Your father was an amazing man, always so kind and generous. I'm going to miss him. I was having difficulty getting pregnant, and you know what your father suggested?"* *"Vitamin C"*, I said mechanically. She looked shocked. *"Why yes. How did you know?"* I wandered off without answering. My dad's recommendation for every ailment was Vitamin C.

Other people looked at me sadly and said things I didn't hear. I nodded. I didn't know what to say. My propensity towards autism kicked in during this time. I was in a daze, but sometimes, at night, I would grip my pillow and cry.

As the mourners began to leave, I noticed a group of women gathered near the church entrance. They were whispering and casting furtive glances towards me. One of them approached me with a young boy in tow. *"I'm Emily. This is my son Ian. Your father was an angel. I can't tell you how much he helped me, not just me. He touched the lives of so many people in ways you can't even imagine."*

Despite my pain and shock, I found comfort in knowing that my dad would live on in the hearts of those he'd touched in the local community.

Returning home was an anticlimax. My aunt left me alone. I spent most of the time in my room, coding, coding, coding, especially at night. I would often look out the window and see dawn coming. Then, I would sleep through until the afternoon. To put it politely, I was obsessed. Coding was my only solace. It was the only thing I felt I could control.

While I was staying with my aunt, a letter arrived, forwarded on from the school. That should have been a moment of joy. I'd been accepted into Emmanuel College, and they understood enough to offer me a year off "*given the circumstances.*" However, I found myself utterly indifferent to the news. I responded with a polite letter that I didn't need a year off and would see them in October.

Two weeks after the funeral, my aunt and I went to see the solicitor. I sat in silence while she did all the talking. I gazed out the window at a tree where two blackbirds were squawking at each other – some fight over territory perhaps, or maybe a mating ritual? I stood up and went to the window to get a better look. My aunt and the solicitor looked alarmed.

"*Sam, this is important. Can you come back here and pay attention.*" My aunt rolled her eyes at the solicitor, who smiled sympathetically. I sat down feeling uncomfortable and bored.

Naturally, my dad had given me everything, with only a few sentimental gifts for his sister. A life insurance policy he'd taken out after my mum's death would provide financial security. Although the car was a complete write-off, it was fully insured. The solicitor had already organised for me to select a replacement "*when I was up to it.*"

As we prepared to leave the solicitor's office, he asked me to wait a moment. While my aunt got the car, he told me that on my father's instruction, he'd already transferred £5,000 to my bank to tide me over and then handed me a sealed letter. "*It's from your father*". I sensed he wanted to say more, but my aunt was waiting. I nodded and tucked the letter into my jacket pocket.

When we got home, my aunt brewed some tea while I took tentative steps in the garden. I made a discovery. I no longer needed my crutches. It was as if the weight of my burdens had been lifted, and I felt a powerful sense of independence returning. I walked back into the kitchen, savouring the moment.

"*I want to go home,*" I declared, surprising myself and my aunt with the strength of my resolve.

"*Don't be silly, Sam. You can't live alone, especially with your leg,*" she reasoned.

"*I'm eighteen, and I've enough money. I want to be home, and my leg is fine,*" I blurted out, my determination evident in my eyes.

It was often the case that I didn't know what I was thinking until I said it. This was one of those occasions. I realised that it was true. I did want to go home. My aunt intuitively recognised this as well. "*Well, in that case, you better sort out a car. We can go to the car yard in town tomorrow*", she said primly.

That night, I had the strangest sleep. I was asleep but alert, as if I was awake. I began to dream. I was standing in a corridor of a hotel with someone who was showing me an assault rifle. I could tell that it was well made, and he was very proud of it, but the guests who walked past were extremely disturbed that someone had a gun in the hotel which they were showing off. Being totally present, I realised that every aspect of the dream was my own invention, the gun, the guests, the hotel, everything. I could change any aspect of it. I turned the gun into a cake and watched the guests' relief. I shrunk the gun owner to the size of a mouse and watched him scurry off. I was no longer a passive viewer but the director of the movie.

When I awoke the next day, I felt more relaxed than I had in years. In minutes, the dream had dissolved like a broken spider web, and I had completely forgotten the letter in my jacket pocket.

6 People actually clapped when I entered the common room.

4: Hal

Geon, the pigeon that has taken up residence in the back garden, has a new phrase. I think he's saying, *"No more milk subsidies. No more milk subsidies. No more milk subsidies"*, like a protestor at a demonstration. It seems strange for a bird to get worked up about an obscure government policy. Still, as one of the last of his kind, he might understand how milk subsidies have impacted his environment. Or he might be barking mad. Whatever the reason, I wish he'd stop. It's annoying.

What do I remember?

Ah, yes, I was alone. I was an orphan—a strange word to use these days. My leg was bent out of shape. And yet, at that time, I was happy. I was so glad to be away from Deerborne. I had time off, money in the bank, a second-hand white and green Mini Clubman, and my new passion – coding. I was liberated from the stranglehold of society and school and felt a freedom that would have been unimaginable a few months ago. Of course, I missed my father. That was an ache that would not disappear quickly.

The first thing I'd done when the money arrived from the life insurance was pay off the mortgage. Now, I owed nothing to anyone. I was free.

You might think it strange that I wasn't lonely. I'd learned to live by myself since I was twelve. I enjoyed the company of others, but I didn't crave it. Besides, I was making friends online. One in particular. Hal. At first, back in June, he'd helped me fix some bugs in my FlightGear code. We never spoke on the phone – always text messaging on Pidgin, a secure chat program. I had no idea where Hal was or what he did for a living. It didn't matter. But Hal was always asking me questions. I remember that gradually and tentatively, I opened up despite it being hard for me. Over the course of a few chats, I told him about my life. Of course, I didn't tell him about Ricky but said I hadn't had close friends at school. I told him about my leg and my father's death. Somehow, I felt he could be trusted and didn't judge me. After a few weeks, he started a new thread.

"*I'm working on this project. I'm trying to create digital money. I could use your help if you're interested*," said Hal.

"*I don't know anything about money, Hal. I just left school. I find money, the economy, and all that completely baffling. We did some economics classes at Deerborne, but they were so boring. I'm not the best person.*"

"*That's OK. In fact, it's why I think you could really help. I need someone who knows little about how a financial system is supposed to work. I need a fresh eye. If you understand what I'm doing, that tells me I'm on the right track.*"

"*I don't know. I'm busy right now. Cambridge just sent me a massive reading list. I'm doing a history degree, which is hard stuff.*" I went off on a tangent about the effects of industrialisation on the family structure. I could tell that he was bored.

"OK. I understand. There is no pressure at all. Please don't hesitate to get in touch if you reconsider."

And we left it at that.

That Thursday evening, the last day of August, I decided to go for a stroll. The sun was starting to go down, so I grabbed my jacket to ward off the evening chill. I walked up the lane and turned off to the high fields. I was home before dark, and as I took off my jacket, I realised that the solicitor's envelope was still in my pocket, unopened.

I made dinner, lit a fire in the living room, and sat down to read it in my father's favourite armchair. It was handwritten in his beautiful script, while mine was an illegible scrawl. I never knew how he did that.

I began to read.

My dear Sam,

You're reading this because I'm dead, assuming my lawyer hasn't accidentally given this to you. I've thought about this a lot, what I would write to you. Now that I'm putting pen to paper, I'm at a loss what to say.

I love you. It sounds trite, I know. Leaving you is the hardest thing I could do, but I've got myself in a bit of a pickle, and I don't know how to get out of it; plus, I'm not going to destroy your life either. I've had a good run, though I must admit I've never really been the same since your mother died.

Once you've read this letter, you must destroy it. If anyone else sees it, then my death will be in vain. Can you do that? Please trust me. I'm sure you'll understand why you must keep this to yourself.

You know, or maybe you don't, I was never very good with money. I've always been more interested in the science side of the pharmaceutical business, and I love helping my customers—maybe a little too much.

After your mother died, sometimes women would come to me desperate to have a child and unable to do so. I used to run some tests, and if I found that it was their partner who was firing blanks, I would offer to help. I can understand that this will come as a bit of a shock to you, but let me assure you that I never took money from them. I think that I'm the father of five children apart from you.

I put the letter down for a moment. There was so much to take in. Who my father was, his secrecy, his stilted relationship with my mother, the strange absence of his presence—now all made sense. To this day, I will never forget the impact this had on me. I picked the letter up again.

The trouble is I'm being extorted, and I've no idea who it is. I'm assuming that one of the husbands found out. I don't have any spare cash lying around, and even if I did, I wouldn't pay up because I know that once you go down that road, there's no end to it. The only thing of value I have is my life insurance policy.

I've decided what I'm going to do. There's a sharp corner on the road to Deerborne at Padstow Gorge. It's a notorious blackspot. Nobody will think that I did this deliberately because it's the direct route. If this comes out, I'll lose the business, our home, my reputation, and everything I ever worked for. I'll leave you with nothing. I can't do that. I can string them along for a month or two at the most. Meanwhile, I'm putting my affairs in order. As you know, I married late. I'm way past retirement age. I've had a good life. One day, if you become a father, you'll understand that nothing matters more than your love for your child.

Live a good life, Sam. I'm sure you will do amazing things. I'm just sad I won't be around to see them.

Your ever-loving father.

Some of the words were blurred. He must've been crying as he wrote it. I added my tears to the paper.

I sat in stunned silence. I read the letter twice more to commit it to my memory until it was burned in my brain. Then I threw the letter in the fire and as the paper crawled and writhed, I saw the words scorching, blackening, gone.

As I went to sleep that night, I realised, "*My father had killed himself over money. He had killed himself so that I would have money. He had killed himself so that the nameless blackmailer couldn't get their hands on his money or harm my prospects."* Money. Money. Money. What a mess.

7 Fashionable Tree

5: Money

I like to go for walks, either alone or with my wife. She's not around at the moment, so I am on my own. People say that Lincolnshire is flat and boring. Let them. It keeps the crowds away. The hills are gentle, it's true. That's ideal for cycling and gentle shuffles. As I walk, I let my mind drift.

My mind would like to see a pattern where none, in fact, exists. As I drift, sunburnt, alone on my raft and mad for water, I recall my parents, though not their most intimate secrets. I could tell you the names of my grandparents but not much else. Beyond that, I cannot even invoke my ancestors by name. I, too, will be lost four generations from now, not even a memory. A bird flies overhead, sizing me up with indifference. If I have great-grandchildren, they will not know my name, what I did or even where I lived. I see great freedom in this obscurity.

~

When I awoke the next morning, my head felt bruised. I went about my day in a fog. I felt incredible guilt. *"I'm responsible for his death. I screwed up. I fucking killed him, just like I killed Mr Grey, and fucked up Ricky, fucked my leg, and fucked up everything else I was any good at in my life."* My thoughts went round and round.

I went for a run, pushing myself to my limits. My leg was still a problem, but I swore, shouted, cursed, and grunted through the pain. Exhausted, I came home and jumped in the shower. Then it hit me while the hot water pummelled my skin. Hal wanted help with his new money idea, and my father had told me to do amazing things. I love programming. It seemed like the perfect combination. I would do something that would really make a difference.

I wrote to Hal and told him I'd thought about it some more and was now happy to help. He was delighted. My father's letter was fresh in my mind. He had made it clear, *"Don't tell anybody."* Nobody else needed to know. I didn't tell Hal why I'd changed my mind, and he didn't ask. We chatted.

"OK, so tell me about your idea."

"You've heard of AI, Artificial Intelligence," Hal began.

"Yes, but it's a bit science fiction. They say it'll be years before it can do anything."

It's funny to think of a world without AI but in 2008, it was still just an idea.

"True. Right now, it can only do specific tasks and is limited. But the time will come when that changes. AI will become a part of everyday life. And when it does, it won't be able to cope with modern banking."

"Why not?" My logical brain struggled with this.

"Because of a whole host of reasons. Banks are open from 9-4, Monday to Friday. That's 35 hours a week, 40 if you are lucky, out of a possible 168 hours. You

can't bank for three-quarters of the week. When AI bots take off, they'll need a bank system that's on every day, every moment."

"But why? I can see AI doing some tasks that humans can't, but why will they need to bank?"

"Because what will happen is we'll delegate tasks to the bots, and just like human workers need to be able to buy and sell their services, so will they."

"OK, I get it. You said there were other reasons."

"Yes. Microtransactions."

"*Microtransactions?*" I echoed, not really getting what he meant. Where the hell is this going?

"Bots must be able to buy and sell their services for a fraction of a cent. That won't work with current banking. You can't sell something under a few pounds or dollars because they aren't set up for it. The bank charge would swallow all the money you made."

"Can't you take some money upfront on a credit card, like a pre-payment electricity meter?"

"You're assuming that the bot can open a bank account, provide a passport, a utility bill, apply for a credit card and load it up."

"I see. It's not as easy as it sounds."

"Banks are meant to know their customers, or at least their name, age, where they live, and what they do. That won't be possible with bots. And we haven't even *dealt with international transfers, exchange rates, and credit. We can leave that for another time. The point is the banking system will never support bots. So, my idea is to create a new kind of digital currency, purpose-built for bots."*

"You said digital?" I interjected.

"Yes."

"Well, hang on, I know I don't know as much as you about the Internet, but one thing I do know is that if I create a program, or a spreadsheet, or a Word file, or anything digital, it's easy and free to make millions of copies. In the real world, if you buy something from me and give me cash, you no longer hold it. The cash passes from your wallet to mine. If you were to make digital money and you send some to me, what's to stop me or you, for that matter, from making multiple copies of the same money?"

"I thought you said you don't understand money."

"I don't. This is just logic," I flushed with embarrassment. It seemed that all of the studying I was doing to prepare for Cambridge was positively affecting my thinking process. It was nice to have it acknowledged.

"It's an excellent point. I think I've figured that out. It's a bit complicated, so we can discuss that later."

"I've one other question. What are you going to call it?"

"*Well, I was thinking of Robotcoin, like coins for AI robots.*"

"*How about NetNotes or BotNotes? Maybe Netcoin or Botcoin? That's easier to say than Robotcoin, and people think of Robots as metal replicas of humans, with flashing lights and clanking limbs. These bots will only ever live on the Internet, as far as I understand.*"

"*I prefer coin to note. Note has several meanings, like a musical note and notepad. Coins are unambiguous. Coins have been used throughout history. Because they're made from metal, they're long-lasting. I prefer Botcoin. Yes, that's good. Let's use that.*"

"*You said it might take years before AI bots needed this. Why bother doing this now?*"

"*Well, you must start sometime, and I think some people will want to use it as well. If we can make it interesting for them, then they can test it out over several years and make sure it really works.*

Let's say it takes fifteen years for bots to become mature enough to want to start using money; I reckon that's sufficient time to iron out the bugs, right? If many people start using it, it'll be pretty valuable in fifteen years' time."

"*Wow! You really think long-term. Fifteen years is most of my life,*" I remarked, but Hal ignored that and changed the subject.

"*By the way, I think you need a new computer. I'm sending one by courier. It's got a lot of the initial code*

I've been working on, plus an updated version of C++. Don't show it to anyone." Hal's proclivity for secrecy was right up my alley. A moment later, he signed off.

8 People say that Lincolnshire is flat and boring. Let them. It keeps the crowds away.

6: Father Christmas

Perhaps Geon was into metaphors. Today, he's repeating the word *"carving"*. Carving, carving, carving. Then occasionally *"literally"*. The milk subsidies campaign is off-topic for now. *"Carving what, Geon? Or carving who?"* I asked. Is it who or whom? I'm never sure. He fixed me with a beady eye as if to say, *"If you can't figure that out, I can't help you"*. I don't think our conversation is going very well. The big news, though, is Geon has a mate. They are smaller, scrawnier, and quieter. What am I going to call them? I think Pi will do. Now, where was I?

Three days later, the following Monday, a courier delivered the computer. It was a top-of-the-range HP xw8600 Workstation. The black tower was fully loaded with Windows XP Professional. The hard drive was an astonishing 160 gig. It even had a read-write optical DVD drive. As promised, C++ and the Botcoin code were fully installed. About an hour after I unboxed it and was reading through the manuals, I got a call from Mike at HP customer support. Mike wanted to know if I needed any help setting up. I felt like royalty. A new fancy computer and support calling me; unheard of at that time. I was confident I could make everything work, but I had a thought before I ended the call.

"Can you tell me the sender's name, Mike?" I asked.

"Sure. One second. It's a Mr. Hal."

"No, Hal's his first name. What's the surname?"

"Sorry. It just says, Mr Hal."

"Can you tell me an address?"

"Sorry, can't do that."

"Privacy reasons?"

"No. I can only see that it's come from California, and we're having trouble syncing our systems. I can get that for you, but it might take some time."

"Could you? I'd be grateful. It's a gift, and I want to thank them, but I've misplaced their address," I requested.

It was troubling me that Hal knew so much about my life, and I knew nothing about Hal. I'd given him my address so he could ship me the computer, but I didn't recall giving him my phone number. So, how did HP support know who to ring? Hal seemed like a nice person, the new computer was amazingly generous, and the project was fascinating, so much so that I'd ditched playing around with FlightGear. I was now fully immersed in Botcoin and reading books about money.

I had always assumed that money was a recent invention. But then I found out that some of the very first examples of writing were ledgers or spreadsheets. I read that archaeologists have found clay tablets in Mesopotamia (modern-day Iraq) dating back to 3400 B.C. They were used to account for grain and workers as part of business, bureaucratic, and personal record keeping. To me, this demonstrated that money predates written language, which is mind-boggling. It means that it is not a technology. It's a part of what it is to be human. I became convinced that money is actually a foundation of human civilisation. Over time, the form has changed, but the basic concept of exchanging something for a token is hardwired. It's the first example of our ability to abstract. You can see it in kids who will create money using anything to hand, stones, cards, sweets, whatever.

I had taken money for granted my whole life, so it was absorbing to ask myself what it is and what makes one form of money good and another bad. Why do some forms of money become obsolete?

Still, I was starting to feel concerned. Who was Hal? Why was he being so mysterious? On a couple of occasions, I'd suggested we speak on Skype, but Hal demurred. At least I now knew that he lived in California. Probably. Possibly.

I thought about the times when we had messaged. I went back through all our conversations. California is eight hours behind most of the year. So, at 7 am, his time, was 3 pm in England. It seemed to fit. He never wrote messages in the morning, my time, meaning he was probably asleep. I knocked up a little Excel spreadsheet and charted the times of all his messages. What I was looking for was a pattern. If he were in California, you would expect clusters of messages when he woke up and then more, perhaps in the evening his time, assuming he had a day job. I looked at the chart. It seemed to fit. There was no way to find his exact location unless he told me, so I dropped it for now. But it rankled that he didn't trust me.

I woke up in the middle of the night. I had had a dream, but it dissolved within seconds. What was it? I let my mind wander as I recalled an incident when I was about five or six years old. It must've been around then because it was before my mum got sick. I remember it was cold walking to school, and I used to wear a duffel coat. That meant it must've been early December. I was in the hall at my primary school playing tag with Tommy Little.

He was a strange boy. He said he liked to sniff petrol, and I had no idea why. He said the smell was great. He looked at me intently, willing me to try it. There was no way I was going to do that. I thought it was horrible. Maybe he was hoping that I would sniff it, and he could watch me and see what would happen. As a child, you just don't know.

A few weeks later, I told my mum. At the time, she was polishing the wooden floors while I sat watching, absentmindedly playing with a puzzle. I loved the hum, the sticky wax's smell and the polishing machine's calm certainty. Have you ever used one? It's a beast to use, and when you switched it on, it would whine and try and snap your wrist, like trying to handle a wayward beast. I was just prattling on, telling her things which had happened, like stuff at school, games I enjoyed, friends I'd made and sniffing petrol. She blanched, turned the machine off, said, "Wait here," and went straight to Tommy's mum. She rang the bell, told her I couldn't play with him anymore, turned around and left. That was my mum, focused and determined.

"*He doesn't exist,*" Tommy asserted.

"*Who? Who doesn't exist?*"

"*You know.*"

"*No, I don't. Who?*"

Tommy looked at me with a gleam of triumph. He knew something I didn't, which was a big deal.

"*Come on, Tommy.*"

"*Father Christmas.*"

I looked at him. Tommy wasn't very bright; clearly, someone had told him a fib.

"*Of course, he exists.*" My anxiety abated. I was on solid ground.

"*No, he doesn't. I overheard my mum and dad talking. He doesn't exist. He's made up.*"

Could this be? Was it possible? No. It was ridiculous.

"*I'm not playing with you,*" I declared firmly and stormed off. He had to be lying. But now I was worried. Not knowing about something that, it seemed, everyone else (even Tommy) did, I was suddenly adrift and uncertain about myself. I knew with absolute certainty that Father Christmas existed. My mum had told me. Every year, Christmas was so exciting. I tried to stay awake to see him arrive, but somehow, I always fell asleep too soon. Then, when I woke up in the morning, there were presents at the bottom of my bed. There was always chocolate and a tangerine. The combination of the two was exquisite. As I peeled the tangerine, it would give off tiny pinpricks of orange. The best was to pop a square of chocolate in my mouth, let it soften and dissolve, and then crush a segment of the tangerine to mingle with the brown sweetness, adding a sharpness to the languid cocoa. I didn't care if I was unable to remove all the pith. It just added texture.

Throughout the day, my mind was in turmoil. If this wasn't true, what else had they lied to me about?

When the school bell rang, I couldn't wait to go home. I pushed past the other kids; I was the first out the door, and in my haste, I even forgot my school bag. I ran most of the way and stormed into the kitchen, where my mother was doing some ironing.

"*Is it true?*" I asked indignantly.

"I*s what true?*" my mother responded, puzzled.

"*Tommy Little says that Father Christmas doesn't exist. You made him up!*" In accusing her, I felt the stirrings of a surge of betrayal.

I saw the shock on my mother's face, and I burst into tears.

"*Come here, darling,*" my mother beckoned, reaching out to hold me close. But I was angry and resisted this rare tender moment with my mother.

"*Why? Why did you lie to me?*" I demanded through sobs.

"*Because I didn't want you to be like Tommy, going around spoiling it for all the other kids,*" my mother explained, her voice softening with understanding.

As an adult, I understand why she did it. She was doing what she thought was right, protecting me.

But the six-year-old me heard something different, darker, more ominous. It never occurred to her that she could've told me the truth, and I would have kept it to myself. No, what I heard was something different.

You can't be trusted.

And here we were a dozen years later, and I still couldn't be trusted. Hal wouldn't tell me who he was or where he was. Well, fuck him. I'm going to find out.

The next day, Mike from HP called.

"*I got that address for you.*"

"*Wait, let me get a pen. OK, ready,*" I replied, preparing to jot down the information.

"*Crema Coffee Roasting Company, 1202 The Alameda, San Jose, California 95126.*"

"*You're sure?*"

"*That's what it says here.*"

I put the phone down. I don't think that Hal runs a coffee shop. I did an online search, and it was owned by a woman named June Tran, who opened the coffee shop last year; she didn't seem to have anything to do with coding, the Internet, or money.

I realised my leg was as healed as it ever would be; I had money and time and always wanted to visit America. My passport had five years left, so I went to London the next day, queued up, got a US holiday visa, and popped into a travel agent who booked my flight from Heathrow to San Jose via San Francisco, leaving the following Friday morning. Based on the agent's recommendation, I decided to stay a couple of weeks at the Westin San Jose. I told Hal I would be out of range on a walking holiday with my aunt in Scotland. I didn't want to alert him to my plan.

At immigration, they grilled me a bit more than I would have liked. "*What is the purpose of your visit?*" the immigration officer inquired. I was unaware that this was a standard question. I thought I was being singled out. I didn't like being under scrutiny, and I couldn't exactly tell him what I was there for.

"Holiday". It seemed a suspicious answer, even to me.

"*Where're you staying?*"

"*At the Westin San Jose.*"

The immigration officer looked at me suspiciously.

"*That's expensive. Show me your proof of reservation.*"

I showed him the details, and he wrote them down.

"*How can you afford that?*"

I was irritated, tired, disorientated by the flight, a little scared, and lost my temper.

"*Two months ago, my father lost control of his car, plunged down a gorge on his way to meet me, and was killed. I don't have any siblings, and my mum died when I was eight. That's how,*" I explained, the words spilling out in a rush of emotion. My lip was trembling. I looked at him defiantly.

It hit me as I blurted it out to this stranger. I'm alone. He looked at me momentarily, deciding whether to escalate to his supervisor. Then, to my great relief, he stamped my passport.

"*Next, in line,*" the immigration officer nonchalantly dismissed me with a wave, signalling for the next person to approach.

I was thoroughly jet-lagged when I checked into the hotel on South Market Street in the late evening. I took a shower and went to sleep, resolving to visit the coffee shop the next day. It was only ten minutes by cab.

The next morning, after breakfast in the restaurant I decided to walk over to the café. It was only half an hour and a fine sunny Californian day. Walking would give me time to think, and it felt good after hours on the plane.

When I arrived at Crema around 10.15, half a dozen people were drinking coffee and chatting. The place felt unpretentious, relaxed, and easy, so I ordered my coffee at the bar and sat at a table near the window. It wasn't an Internet café as such, but several people had laptops and were connected to the café's Wi-Fi. I got the impression that some people used Crema as their office.

I wondered if any of the people there might be Hal and if they were, would they recognise me? I realised that I hadn't thought it through. If he were there, he wouldn't be happy, to say the least. I looked at the people drinking coffee. Nobody was giving me furtive glances. If he was a regular, he wasn't in right now. After a couple of hours of nursing my coffee and reading a book, I left. Maybe I'll strike lucky tomorrow.

~

I was starting to get frustrated and annoyed; I'd returned three days in a row with no luck. The server came over, and I recognised her, as she'd served me a couple of times before. She smiled and was friendly, though we hadn't spoken. She wore jeans and a T-shirt and looked to be about 27 years old. She was tall and gangly and walked with a self-confidence that I didn't feel.

"*Can I get you anything else?*" she asked.

"*You're English. I thought so,*" I remarked.

"*Sort of. My mother's English. My father's American. I was born in England and moved here when I was ten. I live here in San Jose now. My parents are in Frisco. Sorry, am I oversharing? My name is Zoe.*"

"*Yes, your name tag gave it away. I'm Sam. I just arrived a few days ago from England. I can't believe that one of the first people I meet is 'sort of' English.*"

"*What brings you to San Jose?*"

"*I just finished school, so I've time off until October and just started learning to code. Seems like everything happens in Silicon Valley, so I thought I'd check it out.*"

"*What language?*"

"*C++.*"

"*Shut the fuck up. Me too!*" Her eyes lit up, and she gave me a broad smile. I felt an endorphin rush. A fellow coder. I couldn't believe it.

"*So, this isn't a career?*" I said playfully.

"*Of course not. I just started this week. I've no idea what I'm doing, but it pays the rent. I can introduce you to other coders in the Valley if you're interested.*"

"*That would be amazing,*" Suddenly, America wasn't this disconnected place. There was a community, and I could be part of it – through Zoe.

Just then, the barista called Zoe away. I went to the bathroom and, for the first time, noticed a set of letterboxes in the corridor. One of them had the name tag Hal. The box was locked, but I could see that there were a few letters stuffed in. It looked like it hadn't been emptied for a while.

When Zoe came back, I asked her casually about the post boxes.

"Yes, a bunch of customers use here as their address. Heh, I can't really talk right now. I get off at 4. Shall we meet then?"

I went back to the hotel and passed out. This jet lag is strong. I woke up at 9 pm sprawled on the bed with the TV blaring and all the lights on. I'd missed meeting Zoe, and I had no way to contact her. I felt like crap.

9 The server came over, and I recognised her, as she'd served me a couple of times before. She smiled and was friendly.

7: Zoe

I like printed photo albums. I have one from that time. I pulled it from the shelf, opened it, and a photo fell out. I picked it up from the floor with trembling fingers. There's me with Zoe, taken outside Crema on her break. We were so young. The sun is in our faces, so we are screwing up our eyes. Zoe is wearing a Crema apron and laughing at the camera.

I can't remember who took the photo or why. Zoe's pale white skin and black hair glowed. My eyes were full of hope and wonder. At the time, I thought I was so old and mature. Now, I look at this young Sam and wonder how he managed. He's a baby.

~

The next morning, I skipped breakfast and took a taxi to Crema. I immediately spotted Zoe cleaning a table when I walked in.

"*I'm so sorry. I screwed up. I went back to the hotel, lay down for a few minutes, and woke up at 9 pm. It's the jetlag. I don't have your number or email address, so I couldn't contact you. Even if I did, my phone won't work here, and I haven't sorted out the Internet yet,*" I explained, feeling guilty and flustered.

My voice trailed off as I ran out of excuses. She gave me a bright smile.

"*It's totally fine. I finish early today. Do you want to meet for lunch? I'm on Facebook.*" She gave me her account name.

I went back to the hotel. In the lobby, there was a business centre with a couple of computers connected to the Internet. So, I grabbed the login details from reception and opened Facebook. I found her and sent a request to connect. She must've seen it in a break, as she responded almost immediately.

I browsed through her Facebook page. There were photos of her with her parents in the backyard of her house. I noticed that her mum was in a wheelchair. There were photos of her playing guitar at a club, and photos of her kissing and cuddling with what I assumed was her girlfriend on a beach somewhere. She had several hundred connections, far more than me.

At lunchtime, we met outside Crema and walked back towards downtown, ducking into a pizza place that Zoe knew and liked. We talked for hours. We just clicked. Having gone to an all-boys school and not having any sisters, I was surprised by how easily we got on. I even said that.

"*You do realise that girls are people, too?*"

"*I'm sorry. Of course. Stupid of me.*"

"*I'm teasing you,*" Zoe snorted with a playful grin.

I told her about Ricky. It was the first time I'd ever told anyone. I told her about my dad. She told me about her life. When Zoe was 16, her mum had been walking down the street on her way to her car after getting some groceries, and someone took a shot at a rival gang member, missed, and hit her instead. She survived but was paralysed in her lower body. I was aghast. She told me about her music and how she was writing and performing songs at a club. She told me about her girlfriend; they had been together for a couple of years.

The waiter came over to our table. *"We're closing soon,"* he said quietly. I looked at my watch. It was 5.40 p.m., and I couldn't believe how quickly the time had passed. We'd been in such deep conversation. I paid the bill, and we went outside.

We walked and talked, going in no particular direction. We just wanted the flow to continue. It felt easy, friendly, and without encumbrances. I was glad that there was no sexual vibe. We just connected in a way that I'd never experienced before, so on impulse, I decided to tell her about Hal.

"*I'm working on this project. Do you know what the most sellable thing in the world is but is totally useless?*"

"*Give me a clue.*"

"*It's colourless, odourless, invisible. I hinted, " You can't eat, wear, live, or drive in it.*

"*What is it? I've no idea what you're talking about.*"

"*Money.*"

"*Money isn't colourless,*" Zoe objected, taking out a dollar bill. "*See. It's green.*" She sniffed it. "*Eeew. It smells gross.*"

"*That's not money. That's just a piece of paper that represents money. If I give you a photo of a chocolate cake, it's not a chocolate cake.*"

"*OK. I can kind of see your point. When I send you money by bank transfer, it's just electrons. You're right. Money is weird. I've never really thought about it.*"

"*I agree. Yet, it's half of every transaction. Money is the most desirable thing because you can swap it for anything you want, but it's completely useless. We take money for granted. It's just a given. But the more I read, and think about it, you can't have progress without money. Money enables us to trade, which means we can specialise. When we focus on one thing, we get better at doing it. Without money, we are back to barter, and that's primitive. Money is essential to everything we do. It's not the root of all evil, but the root of all goods.*"

Zoe started to tire of the conversation, saying facetiously, "*You could burn it if you had crash-landed on a desert island and were cold or wanted to cook a fish you caught.*"

"*Not if the money was in your bank account. The thing about money is nowadays, it's owned and controlled by the government. They decide how much to print.*"

That got her attention. "*Nowadays?*"

"*Government-controlled money is a 20th-century innovation. Up until then, money wasn't government money. Before paper money, there was gold. Did you *know that in the 1930s, it was illegal for an American to own gold? They passed a law and told everyone they had to hand in their gold, and they got cash back instead. The government took all the gold. Then, a few years later, they changed the exchange rate, so everyone's money was worth less."*

"In America? Are you sure it wasn't Russia?" Zoe questioned.

"Yep. President Roosevelt made it a criminal offence in 1933 to own gold. They only repealed it in 1974."

"I did not know that. Why'd he do that?"

"I'm not sure. I'm still researching and learning. The project I'm working on is to create money that nobody controls, not the government, banks, or big corporations. The idea is to create money that robots will use in the future."

When I said that, it sounded ridiculous, mad, or both, so I tried to clarify.

"Not robots that walk around and serve you coffee, robots on the Internet. Bots, for short."

"Is this your idea?"

"No. God no. I'm just getting my head around it. It's the brainchild of someone called Hal. He thinks that bots will need money to work and that they'll need to create money which is outside of the control of banks and governments."

"Why?"

"Because when a government prints more money, it causes inflation. If a bot provides a service and accepts money in exchange, it needs to know that the money won't decrease in value otherwise, there's no incentive to save, and it's tough to know if something goes up in price because it is more valuable or because there is more money sloshing around in the system. It just messes up the price mechanism."

Zoe thought about this for a moment, digesting it. Then she said, "*Wait. You asked me about a mailbox at Crema. Isn't one named Hal? Is it the same person?*"

Zoe had connected the dots.

"*Zoe. OK, you can't tell anyone about this. This is why I'm here. The thing is, Hal is great. He's really cool. learning so much from working with him. He gave me this amazing computer to work on. But I've never met him, and that worries me. I did some detective work and tracked him down to your coffee shop. Is that wrong? I mean, this could be a mad science project and go nowhere, but I feel like I'm being manipulated.*"

"*No, I totally get it. You just want to know who the dude is. Look him in the eye. Makes sense. I mean, why did he contact you? I mean no disrespect, but I'm a few years older than you. You've no close family or friends. You've just left school. You live alone. You must admit that if you were going to groom anyone to do something, let's say, a little illegal, you're an ideal target.*"

"Where did that come from? *Did you have to say that? Now I feel paranoid.*"

"*I'm sorry, it's just that the government is the only one allowed to print money, and you are talking about making your own.*"

She broke an awkward silence by saying, "*What's the plan?*"

At that point, I realised I didn't have a plan. I was just a kid on an adventure, making it up as I went along.

I hesitated.

"*How do the people who get mail know that something has arrived?*"

"*We don't bother telling them. It's up to them to come and pick it up when they want. We only contact them if they get something too big to put in their box or are overdue on paying the bill.*"

"*Could you get Hal's contact details? You could send him a message saying that a parcel has arrived, and he could pick it up.*"

"*Yes, but then you don't know when he'd turn up.*"

"*I know. You send him a message that there's a courier with a parcel, but he must sign for it and that the courier will be back tomorrow.*"

"*Maybe three days? He might not be in San Jose,*" Zoe suggested.

"*Good idea. Will you do it?*"

"OK. Why not?"

The next day, Zoe told me she found Hal's contact information in a file on her boss's desk in the office out the back. It wasn't a phone number but a Yahoo email address. When her boss was on a lunch break, she used the office computer and sent a quick message to Hal telling him to come at 1 p.m. that Friday.

10 Zoe told me she found Hal's contact information in a file on her boss's desk in the office

8: The Grill

A family of hedgehogs is living at the bottom of the garden. I have no idea how they have survived. When faced with danger, most animals choose fight or flight. Hedgehogs can't do that. They freeze, curling up in a ball so that their spines provide an impenetrable thicket. It's not a bad strategy and one I have adopted over the years, especially in group discussions. I tend to hold my tongue and say nothing if someone powerful says something obnoxious. Still, hedgehogs have been around for at least fifteen million years, so freezing is not a bad strategy – except when you meet a car on a road.

Friday 22nd August 2008

I got to Crema at 12.30, ordered a coffee and sat at the same table I had on the first day I visited. I could see outside, the entrance, and all the customers. Zoe was behind the counter, stacking the washing machine. She'd chosen 1 pm because she knew her boss would be out then, and she could meet Hal.

We had thought about me dressing up as the courier, but that seemed too farfetched.

To distract myself, I was reading an article in *New Scientist* about language and metaphor. I'd always been fascinated by this, but nobody else seemed interested. The article was about the humble preposition. Nouns and verbs get the most attention; their sidekicks, pronouns, and adverbs add meat and colour. According to the article, there were millions of nouns and verbs, and new ones were coined all the time, particularly in science and popular culture. Yet there were less than 200 prepositions, and they'd hardly changed in years. They provided location in space and time for nouns and direction for verbs. I highlighted a sentence that stood out. *"If you think of prepositions, literally pre-positions, as providing coordinates and movement in the four-dimensional models we make of the world, you realise how significant they are."*

One pm came and went. I scanned the other customers. Everyone looked innocent and innocuous. The café was uncharacteristically quiet, so Zoe came over and sat with me for a few minutes.

"*What are you reading?*" Zoe asked as she approached.

"*An article about prepositions,*" I replied. My mind was still in university mode.

"*Seriously?*"

"*It's actually really cool. Say you hear someone talking about 'banging their head against a brick wall,' what do you think is the most significant word in that sentence?*"

"*I don't know. Head? Wall?*"

"*According to this article, it's the word 'against,'* " I explained.

"And w*hy is that?*" I could tell her heart wasn't in the conversation. She was anxious about Hal walking in, and wondering why he was late.

"Well, think about it. It's a metaphor for someone's frustration. They can't achieve what they want. It's pointless and painful. If you change the phrase to 'banging your head over a brick wall,' or 'behind a brick wall,' it loses its meaning,"

"*And?*" Zoe urged me to continue, to seem natural if Hal walked in.

"*And, if you make a teeny tiny change by replacing one preposition for another, you can transform your understanding of the world.*"

"*Give me an example.*"

"*People talk about freedom, especially here in America. You're so obsessed with freedom, and yet you all want to walk around with guns.*"

"*Yes, the right to bear arms is in the constitution.*" She seemed prickly.

"*The right to bear arms, not to walk around with sub-machine guns. You, of all people, should know how nutty that is. You know it's ten times more dangerous in America than the UK and that most deaths from shootings happen in the home. Anyway, let's not go into that.*

My point is this. If someone says they want freedom, the question is, do they want freedom to or freedom from? They aren't the same thing at all. If you want freedom from, you'll never get it. Freedom to, excludes the problem. That one subtle change can transform the way you see the world."

"*That's interesting. You're a very peculiar person, Sam. But I have to work. Keep an eye out,*" Zoe replied before attending to a customer.

After another hour, I gave up. He wasn't coming. I went and paid Zoe. I decided to go outside to get some fresh air. I noticed three well-dressed men in suits and ties getting out of a car and approaching Crema. As they were about to pass, one grabbed my neck, another tripped me up, and I landed hard on the concrete. It happened so quickly that I was in shock, and within seconds, my hands were behind my back and cuffed.

"*Don't fucking move!*" one of the men, an agent I supposed, commanded. That seemed a pointless thing to say as I couldn't move even if I wanted to. I felt the cold concrete pressing on my cheek.

"*What's happening?*"

They bundled me into the back of the car, and we drove off in a sickly silence. I don't think it was more than ninety seconds from when I walked out the door. I turned around, and I glimpsed Zoe standing there through the rear window, looking utterly perplexed.

I was taken to an FBI office building on the outskirts of San Jose. I was photographed, fingerprinted, and put in a cell for three days. Nothing happened, apart from food being delivered. The following Monday, I was taken to a small room on the fifth floor. There was no furniture except for a mirror, table and two chairs. The only photo was an official portrait of George Bush, the outgoing president. I tried the door. It was locked. I stood at the window, still in shock. Outside, I saw cars on the freeway. Because of the thick security glass, the scene was silent. A normal day. Everyone was going about their business while I watched, suddenly disconnected and very alone.

The door opened. A man walked in holding a thick manila folder, a legal pad, and a pen. I could see my name written in black pen on the folder cover. He sat down.

"*I'm Special Agent Tom Massini. Take a seat,*" Tom instructed as he entered the room.

As I took my seat at the table, a knot of apprehension tightened in my stomach, a physical manifestation of the tension in the room.

"*Why am I here?*" I questioned.

"*I have the same question. Why are you here, Sam? Why did you fly from the UK and go straight to Crema the day after you arrived? Why've you been befriending—*" he glanced at the folder "*—a server there called Zoe Bridge? You're here on a tourist visa for two weeks, but you don't seem to be seeing the sights, visiting friends, you know, the normal things tourists do.*" He looked at me quizzically, and I wondered what was in the folder. I could see the edge of the papers. Something was odd. I forced myself to breathe slowly.

"Why don't you tell me what you want?" I deflected, attempting to maintain a facade of calm. I extended my hand to shake his, a friendly and calculated gesture. In the process, I 'accidentally' knocked his pen to the floor. As he bent to retrieve it, I seized the opportunity to glance at the folder. My suspicions were confirmed, but the contents only deepened the mystery. A single typed sheet of paper with my name, travel details, and a photo of me taken at immigration in San Francisco. The words Zoe Bridge, Crema, and Hal caught my eye, but I didn't have time to read the notes. The bulk of the folder was a blank paper pad, a stark contrast to the weight of the situation.

I babbled nervously to deflect.

"Sorry about that. Clumsy. Look, my father died recently, and I felt the need to get away. I met Zoe purely by accident. I didn't know her before. I've never travelled before, except for small trips to France. This jet lag is a shocker. It's taken a few days. I was going to start doing the sights tomorrow. What's this all about?"

"Sam, please don't play dumb. We know you came to meet Hal. We know you got close to Zoe to get to him."

A moment later, the door opened, and a man came in, whispered something in Tom's ear, and left. Tom turned bright red and looked at me furiously.

"You looked at my file! That file is the property of the US government. That's a felony!"

"I don't think it's illegal to drink coffee. I don't think chatting with a waitress is banned in the US. I don't think looking at an empty paper pad is a criminal offence. False imprisonment is. That door is locked. I can't leave. Either you charge me with something, or you can fuck off. I'm not going to answer any of your questions."

Tom left, and I was alone for the rest of the morning.

~

I held the photo of Zoe and me outside Crema. It was the last time that I could say my life was normal. I remember thinking that if Tom thought he could intimidate me, he hadn't spent seven years in an English public school. I knew that the best thing for me to do was nothing. Zoe had seen me being arrested. I remember hoping that she was finding a lawyer to get me out.

Of course, I didn't realise it at the time, but behind the mirrored glass was a multi-agency, multinational team. The FBI was the lead agency, but there were also representatives from the Financial Crimes Enforcement Network, a department within the US Treasury. The IRS Criminal Investigation Unit was there. The Federal Reserve was there. Even the Secret Service was there, tasked with combatting counterfeit currency.

Later, I found out that people from the UK, including HM Revenue and Customs, the Financial Conduct Authority, the Serious Fraud Office, and the Serious Organised Crime Agency, were flown in over the weekend. The Brits took financial crime seriously.

I think I will try to find out where the hedgehogs are sleeping. They are night creatures.

~

The team sat at tables, reading reports about Botcoin and trying to figure out what would happen if it got released into the wild. Special Agent Davis took charge.

"The problem is that Sam is not the ringleader. I think he knows quite a bit, but without Hal, we're stuck."

James Cleverly, from the Serious Fraud Office, had flown in over the weekend, missing his wife's birthday celebration. He was in a foul mood.

"Exactly. I don't understand why you arrested Sam. You thought he was going to crack easily. Instead, he made a laughingstock of Tom. Sorry, Tom, no disrespect. We've come all this way, and as far as I'm concerned, it's been a wasted trip," Cleverly expressed frustration.

Tom glowered in a corner.

"We're blown. Hal has been covering his tracks, and now we're back to square one," Cleverly continued, his tone grim.

"*It was worth the risk. Who knew an eighteen-year-old kid would be so tough? You can't always get it right,*" Davis defended their actions, trying to salvage the situation.

As the meeting concluded, a few less experienced agents wondered why all the fuss was happening. They thought it was a little over the top but were too junior to speak up. They figured that the FBI was worried that this could start a way for criminals to transfer funds globally and bypass banks and all the government's mechanisms to track and trace money movements. Davis seemed determined to nip it in the bud and make life hell for anyone and everyone involved.

At lunchtime, two agents drove me to the hotel, where my bags were loaded into the car, and then directly to San Francisco airport. The journey passed in silence. They put me on a direct flight back to Heathrow. I arrived blurry-eyed at 7 a.m. I was paranoid that I would be arrested on arrival, but nobody paid me any attention. Two hours later, I was back home. The first thing I did was open my computer.

All my messages with Hal, and the Botcoin code, were gone.

11 Horse Tree

9: The Approach

I couldn't find the hedgehogs. They were too well concealed, and my eyes too blurry. I asked Geon, but he didn't know. Pi, well, I don't have a speaking connection with her yet. Maybe I will stay up tonight and see if I can spot them coming out.

I remember feeling that it was over. I was home and safe, but I didn't feel safe. My life was starting to have meaning, purpose, and direction, and now I was a nervous wreck.

~

That Friday, a security expert I'd hired came to sweep my house for bugs. They found nothing. I told them to check the car as well. Nothing. I'd also hired a computer expert to check my computer. They arrived just as the security guy left. Could they restore the code? No. Did I make a backup? No. I hadn't got around to that. Hal had asked me not to.

The one good thing to come out of all of it was meeting Zoe. I contacted her as soon as I was home to tell her I was safe and well. She said she'd been frantic but didn't know where I was or who had taken me. She got her dad to make enquiries, and they finally traced me to being arrested by the FBI, but by then, I was back in England. We spent hours on the phone chatting about everything and nothing.

Whatever Hal was developing must have struck a raw nerve. But why? We had no clue. First, we decided to find out everything we could about the emerging area of artificial intelligence and pool what we learned. A few days later, we compared notes.

"*Well?*" asked Zoe.

"*I'm beginning to understand why Hal thinks it's a big deal. Technology is the base layer of human civilisation. And this AI thing is a pretty big step change,*" I replied.

"*What do you mean?*"

"*Think about any piece of new technology. Before it's introduced, people live their life a certain way. Afterwards, they reorganise. The innovative technology means they can live and work differently,*" I elaborated.

"*For example, the PC revolution.*"

"*Yes. It created thousands of new businesses and destroyed old industries. Technology creates new ways of working. New ways of working change culture. Culture is just a fancy word for 'how we do things around here.' Culture changes politics, which in turn changes laws and regulations. It all starts with technology. Without innovation, we live as our parents did and their parents before them.*"

"*That's true.*"

"*Here's the thing: Until AI, someone designed and built a new piece of technology. If it breaks or gets old, humans repair or replace it.*"

"You mean that every piece of technology is just a tool. It allows us to do more, but it depends on us. It can't learn or adapt," Zoe clarified.

"Exactly. It doesn't matter if it's a nuclear power station or a socket wrench. We decide what the technology will do. The socket wrench can't morph into a screwdriver. But AI is different. It can figure things out without our help. It can understand things which it has never seen before."

"Holy crap!"

"Holy crap, indeed. Well put. Right now, it's clunky and primitive. There's no such thing as general intelligence. It's still designed to work in one specific area. For example, they are using AI for spam filters. It can look at a new spam email that it has never seen before and know it's spam. There are some researchers working on speech recognition. You can teach it the basic grammar rules, and it can begin to understand words and phrases it has never heard before."

"So, what you're saying is that it can understand patterns and rules and extrapolate from there?"

"Yes. And this is going to go exponential. It'll learn something, adapt, learn something, adapt; on and on."

"*So, exponential?*"

"Yes. An exponential curve starts off flat and stays flat for a long time, and then suddenly – whoomph! If we project forward into the future, then this is what I can see happening. Many small groups of researchers will

work on AI to solve specific problems. Computers will get more powerful. I see this cloud thing as the future. You just have to look at how many people have shifted to Google Mail."

"I agree, Sam. And Amazon's web services. It's really the same as what they've done for online shopping. They're eliminating the need for a business to buy servers, host them, get an IT team, and manage them. It's much cheaper and faster.

If we project that trend forward, everyone will eliminate local data storage. It will all go into the cloud, and when that happens, it will all be in one place."

We sat silently for a moment, contemplating the enormous change that was about to come. Zoe added:

"The AI people need tons of data. The more they have, the more powerful the AI becomes. The cloud will deliver that.

"Agreed. Any news from Hal?" I asked.

"Nothing. I assume nothing at your end, either. Did I tell you that Hal has closed his post box? I looked, and he never picked up the last of his mail. I snuck a peek when my manager was out. It was just circulars and a subscription to Wired magazine," Zoe revealed. *"I think it's done,"* she added.

10: Arrival

My wife is a well-known personality, although she hates the notoriety; I'm sure you've heard of her and would recognise her name if I mentioned it. She travels worldwide, giving talks and doing shows about gardening, which is why I haven't mentioned her before; she hasn't been around. That's why I've been talking to pigeons and looking for hedgehogs. She has just returned from a trip to Australia to promote her latest book on edible plants. I'm immensely proud of her and everything that she has achieved. She's a very private person and hates being in the spotlight, but she feels her work is too important for her shyness to get in the way.

I have a publicity shot the magazine sent me. For a woman in her late eighties, she looks amazing. I love her strength and the experience etched into her face. I have it on my bedside table when she's gone.

~

A week later, my computer pinged.

"*Hello, Sam,*" said Hal.

I froze for a moment. I didn't know how to respond. What are you meant to say in these circumstances?

"*Hi,*" I managed to reply.

"*Now, do you understand?*"

"*Understand what?*"

"*Why I asked you not to tell anyone. Money isn't just an everyday convenience. It's power. If you control money, you control the world. What happened to you in San Jose should explain why I don't want to meet in person.*"

"*You knew about that?*"

"*Of course. Can we agree that you won't try to find me?*"

"*Yes, absolutely.*"

"*What about Zoe?*"

"*I trust her. She's also a C++ coder. We've been learning about money and bots together. I'd like to have her on the team. I think she has a lot to offer.*"

"*Very well. I think she'll help you understand more than you realise. She has a quite different perspective from yours. Check your computer.*"

I checked and typed that the Botcoin code was back.

"With some improvements. It must be obvious to you that I've control of your computer. There's code that will block you from making a backup of Botcoin. I've also read all your messages with Zoe. I'm telling you this, so you know how things are. If you don't want to work together, I'll understand. I'm only doing this because I must. I don't think you really appreciate how important this work is yet. It's going to change the world, and that means a lot of people are going to be upset. I'm not going to spend the rest of my life in prison because of someone else's mistakes. You're new in this game. I've been doing it longer than you can imagine. Is that fair?"

"Yes."

"We'll meet. But it'll be on my terms. I'll decide when and where and ensure you and Zoe aren't followed."

"So, Zoe is on the team?" I inquired, hopefully.

"Yes, Zoe is on the team, but you can't send her the code. You can text her the ideas and principles on Pidgin. Don't use Skype, Facebook, or any other way of communicating. No phone calls. Every phone call between England and America is recorded and listened to."

"Seriously?"

"Absolutely. I know this for a fact. Friends of mine worked on the AI keyword searches they use to flag conversations for further analysis."

I was elated. We were still moving forward! Giddy with excitement, I sent Zoe a message to install Pidgin so we could message securely.

"*Have you been working on the Botcoin thing lately?*" Zoe messaged.

"*Yes. Pretty intensely.*"

"*Could I get a copy of the code?*" she asked. It seemed like an innocent question. I hesitated.

"*Sorry. Hal said he and I are the only ones who can have it now.*"

"*Bum,*" Zoe responded.

"*I can summarise where we've got to if you want.*"

"*No, that's OK,*" she declined, then paused. "*Maybe if you could explain what a wallet is, that would be good.*"

"*The wallet is like a digital safe. It stores your coins and your keys. When you create a wallet, you generate a public-private key combination. You use the private key to sign transactions. That proves you own the coins. Everyone else on the network can verify that it's you with your public key.*"

"*Where is that data stored?*"

"*In a file on your computer, wallet.dat.*"

"*What if the file gets lost or corrupted?*"

"You have to make a backup. If you don't, you could lose it."

"That's a bit of a worry, Sam."

"Yes, I agree. It's just the first version; everyone playing with it will be computer-savvy. If this takes off, we'll need to improve the user interface. It's all command-line right now, so you must know what you're doing."

"Fair enough. As you say, if it takes off, we'll need to make a graphic user interface. We can't expect a lot of users if it's too technical and nerdy. She paused for a second.

I suppose they can only get coins if they mine them?" Zoe queried.

"Initially. But the miners can gift them to other people so that they can get a stash and play around with it. Remember, we aren't doing this for people but to get enough users on board to test it out and iron out the kinks. It's really about the bots, and they don't need a graphic interface."

"Yes, I still don't really get that. It feels too far in the future. I don't see why we can't create what you might call private money for people. Many people send money home from abroad, and the charges are outrageous."

"True, and there are loads of people who can't get a bank account or have their accounts frozen in countries run by dictators. When we release it, it

doesn't matter what our plan is. People will start using it in ways that we didn't intend. That's always what happens."

~

A week later, Hal sent me a message.

"I think it's time to meet. Contact Zoe and ensure she has a passport and can travel. I'll let you both know where and when."

I pinged Zoe on Pidgin.

"Your passport up to date?"

"Yes. Why?"

"Hal's arranging for us to meet."

"When?"

"I don't know when or where yet."

"But what about visas? I don't have a UK passport."

"Assuming we meet somewhere in the UK or Europe, you don't need a visa. I checked. Americans are part of the visa waiver program. You can get on a plane if you've at least three months left on your passport. Can you get time off work?"

"Probably."

"I'm assuming it'll be all last minute."

A few days later, Zoe said she'd received a return ticket in the mail that morning. She was leaving in two days to go to Paris, France. I wondered why Americans always say Paris, France. Nobody would fly to Paris, Texas. It was strange because I hadn't received anything from Hal. I messaged him.

"I see that Zoe is going to Paris. Should I book a train on Eurostar?"

"Wait on that for the time being. I've got it all under control. Just be ready to travel tomorrow. I'll send you instructions later today. I have to sort a few things out."

The next day, following instructions, I took the train to London and then the underground to Edgeware. Hal had told me to get in either the first or last car.

At Edgeware, I waited until the very last moment and then jumped off just as the doors closed. I'd an unobstructed view of the station and was certain nobody else had left after me. I exited the station, turned down a side road and found the bike chained to a railing. I'd memorised the combination, but the lock was difficult, and it took me a few goes before it released.

There was nobody in the street. Hal had told me to pack light and to use a backpack, making it easier as I climbed on and cycled a couple of miles north. The traffic was busy, so I used the pavement most of the time. I turned off at the top of the hill and saw the black taxi waiting. "*Sam?*" The taxi driver said. "*Yes,*" I replied. "*Give me a moment.*" I locked the bike to a lamppost and climbed in. The taxi took me a few miles further north and stopped in a layby. I paid and walked down a sideroad to where a green Volvo was parked. I reached under the front wheel arch and found the car key in a magnetic holder, just as Hal had told me where it would be. The drive up the M1 to Birmingham was uneventful. I didn't stop until I came to the NCP car park a few minutes from the station. I parked, walked into the station, and boarded the train to Wales. When I arrived at Machynlleth, I was the only passenger who had gotten off. The taxi driver was waiting for me as expected. Fifteen minutes later, I was at the cottage and found the key under the flowerpot to the right of the door.

Meanwhile, Zoe landed in Paris without incident and was met by a chauffeur who took her bag. She sat in the back of the black Mercedes.

"*Welcome to Paris, Zoe. My name's Gaston. There's a bottle of water if you're thirsty. Please make yourself comfortable.*"

"*Do you know where we're going?*"

"*Right now, we're making our way to the city centre. I'm waiting on a text message with the address.*"

Half an hour later, as they approached the outskirts, Gaston told her that he had an address now and that they should be there in 40 minutes. Zoe noticed that he kept glancing in his mirror.

"*Is everything OK?*"

"*I'm just checking on who is following us.*"

"*We're being followed?*"

"*Definitely. I've spotted one of the cars, but I'm just looking to see if there's another one. Would you mind putting on your seatbelt? I may need to make a few sudden moves.*"

"*OK.*"

As they approached the next freeway turnoff, Gaston suddenly veered off. A car that had been following him was too late to make the turn. It screeched to a halt on the hard shoulder and started reversing at high speed to the exit.

"*Ok, that's one of them. There's a change of clothes in the bag on the floor. Put them on now, please. And give me your phone.*"

While she did, Gaston accelerated away, through back streets, until he came to his destination. On the way, he tossed Zoe's phone into the back of a flatbed truck while waiting for traffic lights to change. Zoe said nothing.

"*Sorry about your phone. You can get a new one. Zoe, we're going to switch cars in a second. I'm going to pop the trunk. Grab your bag and follow me. Are you ready?*"

Gaston didn't wait for an answer. He pulled behind a Blue Fiat and jumped into the driver's seat.

"*Come on!*"

Zoe grabbed her bag, threw it in the back of the Fiat, and jumped in beside Gaston.

"Put this scarf and sunglasses on, please. There's an envelope in the seat pocket. Open it."

Gaston drove off slowly and sedately into the oncoming traffic. He checked his mirror and was confident that they were not being followed. Still, he took a circuitous route to Gare du Nord. In the envelope, Zoe found a UK passport with her photo and the name Zoe Brown, a return ticket on the Eurostar to London, Waterloo, leaving in an hour, five hundred pounds in cash, and a train ticket from London Euston to somewhere called Machynlleth. Zoe had no idea where that was.

"How'd you organise all this?"

"Oh, I didn't. I don't know who did. You get on the Eurostar; when you get to London, get a taxi to Euston station and please don't make any phone calls or use a computer. According to the timetable you'll have about an hour before the train to Machynlleth. Remember to change at Birmingham."

"Where?" Zoe questioned. The town was unfamiliar.

"Machynlleth. It's a small town in Wales near Snowdonia. When you get there, look for the taxi driver with a signboard saying Zoe. He'll take you to your final destination. Good luck."

With that, Gaston helped her with her bag and drove off into the Parisian traffic. Zoe arrived at Machynlleth around 8 pm. The taxi driver was a local and took her out of town, down some country lanes, until they arrived at a small cottage surrounded by fields full of sheep. As they arrived, the outside light came on. Sam stood at the door.

"Hello, Zoe. Long time no see," I greeted her.

The next few days, we went for walks, played Scrabble, and discussed Hal's progress on the code.

It was a crisp September Monday morning. They were starting to get a little frustrated when they heard the sound of a car crunching on the gravel. The engine stopped. They opened the front door to see a man in his early thirties getting out.

"*Morning. My name's Hal,*" he said, walking around to the car's boot to unload it.

12 Shy Tree

11: Bittersweet

I only have one photo of Hal. I took it surreptitiously on my iPhone and emailed it to myself because he didn't like being photographed. I never told anyone about it, but now these events are long past.

I've always been a bit of a tech junky and had picked up one of the very first iPhones released the year before using some of the money my father had left me.

You can't see Zoe because she has her back to the camera, listening to something Hal is saying. She's smoking a cigarette. I'd forgotten that she did that occasionally. They are sitting in the living room, in the cottage in Wales. The light isn't good, but you can make out a mirror on the wall, and if you look closely, you can see me taking the photo.

There are coffee cups and computers on the table. Hal is not tall but muscular, squat, and commanding. His hair is closely cropped like he's been in the army. He's very fit and wearing a dark blue button-down shirt and jeans. He's clean-shaven. His jaw juts out, and his nose looks like a boxer, slightly bulbous like he's been in a few fights.

It might be the only photo of him still in existence.

~

Hal brought three computers from the car, like the one he'd bought me, and set them up in the living room. We made lunch together: pasta and red wine, with a green salad. As we sat drinking our wine, Hal decided to check that we were all on the same page.

"We'll start looking at the code and doing some testing tomorrow, but let's go back to basics. We're creating a new form of money so that bots can do business with each other. You've read about money, so this should be an easy one. What are the three basic properties of money? Sam?"

"Store of value, means of exchange, unit of account," we both chimed in unison. It was a phrase we knew.

"Correct. Zoe, what does 'store of value' mean?"

"When you work you sell what you've produced through your time and effort to someone who wants or needs what you've created. They give you money which you can store until you need to buy something. When you do spend it, it should have the same value as when you first got it. But in practice, money tends to decline in value over time."

"Yes. And why does it decline over time? Sam?"

"Because modern money is owned and controlled by governments. Governments get money in one of three ways. They tax, they borrow, or they print. Taxing is unpopular. Borrowing can be challenging. But printing is easy. If you double the number of notes in circulation, then it's logical that each is worth half. That's what causes inflation."

"Good. So, that's the first problem we want to solve. We want to create a store of value that can't be inflated away. Take me through 'means of exchange.' Zoe."

"Before the Internet, if I wanted to send a letter to Sam in England, I'd write it, put it in an envelope, purchase a stamp, and post it. Now, with the Internet, I just write him an email; it costs me nothing, and he gets it in seconds. The bots we're talking about won't have any physical existence. We want to create a way for them to send and receive money as easy as sending an email."

"That's a great analogy. And 'unit of account?'"

"Most currencies are divided into one hundred units. Dollars and cents, pounds, and pence. We know that the bots will be doing microtransactions, so we've decided that instead of a hundred sub-units, we'll use a hundred million."

"Which means that even if one Botcoin eventually reached a million dollars, you can still do a one-cent transaction."

"Do you think that will happen, get to a million dollars?" I inquired.

"Probably. Maybe. I don't know, but it's just zeroes, so why not future-proof? It's easy to do at this point. It would be ridiculously hard to change it later. Botcoin must be a digital store of value, a means of exchange, and a unit of account."

The next morning, Hal put up some butcher's paper on the walls with Bluetack.

"*Writing code is about solving problems. What problems are we solving?*"

"*We want money that bots can use. That means it must be Internet money and out of the government's control to prevent it from being inflated,*" replied Zoe. Hal wrote these points on the wall.

"*Is it just governments we're worried about?*" questioned Hal.

"*No. Any central body could control the money. That's why our code is 'decentralised',*" I explained. *Let's not forget why the Internet is the way it is. It started off as a thought experiment. How could the US military continue to communicate if there was a nuclear strike that destroyed headquarters?*"

"*That's right. If some bot controls the ledger, they can increase the money supply and cause inflation. They can also decide who's allowed to use the money. If a bot is doing a task that they don't agree with, they can block it. They can also put in place rules and regulations before a bot can start trading. That's going to be slow and inefficient. The more I thought about it the more I realised that the system must be decentralised. We've solved one problem but created another. How do we create a financial system with no central authority? How do we stop inflation? How do we create digital money that can't be duplicated? Let's break it down. I think we've a solution to most of these problems. I'm not the first person to try and figure this out,"*

"OK, let's try it. We've three computers we can use to represent three different Bots. Let's try creating some users, and transactions and see if it works."

"Before we do that, Hal, I want to take stock. We've been talking about this so much I feel I've lost the overall picture. Can I try to summarise what we're doing, why we're doing it, and how it actually works? Then tell me if you think I've missed anything important," I interjected.

"And I'll add anything I think you've missed, as well," said Zoe.

"Good idea. Go ahead. See if you can keep it short and sweet."

I took a moment to reflect.

"We're creating a financial system for bots because, for a whole bunch of reasons, the current system is antiquated and can't be fixed. Bots won't be able to survive or thrive in this system. They won't even be able to open an account. It's better to start fresh. Then, we can make a system that any bot can use to transfer funds, even microtransactions, to any other bot anywhere in the world instantly and easily over the Internet. Because it's decentralised, it's censorship resistant, meaning any bot can create an account. They don't need to ask anyone's permission, and nobody can stop them from doing business. Every bot has their own

wallet, so no bank or government can freeze their account or steal their funds. Because it's decentralised, we've solved the problem of the government banning it or arresting the founders. They can try, but it'll be extremely hard to do."

"That's a pretty good summary of what Botcoin is, and why it exists, Sam." acknowledged Hal.

"What about how it works?" queried Zoe. Hal jumped in.

"I think there are a few key ideas. Modern money has been taken over by governments. Because they can print money, and because that's always an easier option than taxing people or borrowing, the entire system is inflationary. The way we've done that is to cap the total number of Botcoins at 21 million. That means the value over time will never go down, only up.

We've created a class of users we're calling miners, although in truth, they are auditors. Their job is to add new transactions to the ledger every ten minutes. It's a lottery and only the winner is allowed to do that. They get a reward of 50 Botcoins. When the winning miner announces the new block, all the nodes check that it's valid, so they can't fiddle it. For every 210,000 blocks added, this reward is halved. That's about four years. That means most of the Botcoins will be released early."

"And they also get a small fee from the bots with new transactions," I added.

"*Right. And Sam, you came up with a clever idea of ensuring that even without a time server or any central authority, the release of the new Botcoins remains at around ten minutes,*" acknowledged Hal.

"*Which we called the difficulty adjustment, and we do that every 2,016 blocks or two weeks or so,*" Zoe said.

"*And the last key point, I think, is proof of work. The big challenge with a digital asset is how easy it is to make millions of copies. Proof of work solves that problem. You must invest time, effort, and equipment to participate in the mining lottery. Digital sweat. There are no shortcuts,*" I explained.

Zoe had a thought. "*I've a question. These miners. They can be located anywhere in the world?*"

"*Yes,*" said Hal.

"*And they'll all have the same or similar computers,*" she continued.

"*Agreed.*"

"*I'm thinking aloud, so bear with me. So, over time, there'll be an arms race. One miner will get a faster computer, and every other miner will have to match it, or else they'll lose out,*" she posed.

"*True.*"

"*And every four years their profit margin will be cut in half.*" She paused. "*Seems like a crappy business to be in. You've no competitive advantage, no barrier to entry, and your margins get squeezed,*" she concluded.

"*Yes. Everything you say is true, but I think you've overlooked a couple of things,*" replied Hal. "*The first is that over time if everything goes according to plan, more and more miners will join the system. Although their margins will get squeezed, and they'll have to upgrade their hardware continually, if they are smart, they should be able to stay in business. But the second point is that their main cost will be electricity, which doesn't cost the same. Some places have ample electricity so the price will be cheaper.*"

"*OK. That was the other thing I wanted to say. If there's an arms race and more and more miners join, and they use more and more computers, won't that have an adverse effect on electricity? They'll take power away from other users, increasing the price. And what about the environmental impacts? That worries me,*" she added.

"*No,*" said Hal.

"*What do you mean, no?*"

"*What will happen is the miners will seek out the cheapest form of electricity. They can mine anywhere, so they aren't going to do it in a city centre. They'll find power sources which nobody wants because they can park themselves in the middle of nowhere.*"

"*Like what?*" I jumped in.

"*Landfills,*" said Hal. "*They produce methane from the rotten food that gets dumped there. Often the gas floats up into the sky. That's terrible for the environment. It's *way more of a problem than carbon dioxide. I predict you'll see miners setting up in landfills and burning the methane to produce electricity. If that happens, then Botcoin mining will cut carbon emissions."*

"*Great question, Zoe. Shall I continue?*" I asked.

"*We've eliminated trust and replaced it with consensus. We use consensus to check that the ledger is in a perfect state every ten minutes. The only way to change anything we've done is if almost everyone agrees. The miners are important, but they don't have full control. If they want to make a change, they'll have to convince all the nodes that double-check every transaction. That's going to be extremely hard, deliberately so. We want to ensure that some small but powerful group could never change the protocol at some point in the future.*"

"*You mean like increasing the hard cap beyond 21 million?*" I queried.

"*Exactly. That would be a disaster. I think we've made that impossible,*" confirmed Hal.

"*But surely there are bound to be good changes, which not everyone will agree to,*" Zoe pointed out.

"*That's why we're making it open source. Anyone can make a copy and edit it. Then, all the users can decide which version they prefer. Only one will succeed, and the other will wither and die,*" explained Hal.

"*They don't have to try changing the Botcoin protocol, which will be extremely hard. They can also add another layer on top of Botcoin,*" I added.

"*Exactly,*" agreed Hal.

"*Sam, remember you told me about hashing and the blockchain? You haven't mentioned that,*" said Zoe.

"*You're right. That was deliberate. I think it's too much detail. You and I can talk about that later again if you want. All we need to say is that we use well-known cryptographic techniques to ensure that as a new block is added, there's no possibility of it, or any previous block, being changed. I don't think we need to go into how that's done,*" I reasoned.

13 Bear Tree

12: Unexpected Guests

I didn't sleep well last night; I had a nightmare that woke me up. I was in a Victorian house, and we expected to be attacked. Someone decided that we would trick them and pretend that our leader was dead. In dreams, there is no critical analysis. You don't question who the leader is, where you are, or what you do. You arrive midway in the story. Who is attacking us and why? You have no clue, and you don't question it. It just is. Anyway, this blurry person staged an elaborate death in the next-door room. I heard a scream. I rushed in to see the leader's throat being slashed. I couldn't tell if it was real or fake. It looked very real to me. I could see the blood gushing and the look of horror in his eyes.

I woke up in a cold sweat and couldn't get back to sleep. I felt the warmth of my wife lying next to me, breathing slowly and rhythmically. I wanted to reach out to her but didn't want to disturb her.

Maybe I should take a break from remembering these events. Even after all these years, I still find them disturbing. As in a Greek tragedy, you know what's about to happen but can do nothing.

~

Over the next two days, we worked with unwavering focus, meticulously finding and fixing bugs until we were confident it was flawless.

That evening was a celebration. Hal brought out a battered violin. Zoe sang, and I bashed on an upturned kitchen dustbin to provide a beat. We drank too much wine, laughed, and celebrated. We had done it. We had invented digital money that any Bot could create and acquire. They didn't need anyone's permission. They could hold it themselves. There was no intermediary, so nobody could take a commission, block a transaction, or close an account. It was neutral money outside anyone's control. With a fixed supply and release rate, it was the first truly hard money that couldn't be inflated away. In the physical world, you could never say how much money there was. There was no register of every bit of gold mined, and nobody could say how much would be found in the future. Botcoin was the first finite asset ever created.

"*Hal. What's the next step?*" I asked during a lull in the conversation.

"*I want to conduct more extensive testing over the next few weeks, and then we can publish a whitepaper and invite comments. Once that's done, we'll release it open-source. This will demonstrate our commitment to transparency and community involvement.*"

He had said this before, and I had let it pass, always just going along with it. But it bothered me. "*You've been so careful to keep the code a secret. I'm really surprised you want to make it open-source. Why would you do that? Wouldn't that mean anyone can copy it?*"

"*I always intended to release it open source. Remember, we are trying to eliminate trust. If we own the code, everyone else has to trust that we haven't made any mistakes and that we haven't put some secret *trap door in. If they find mistakes, they can help fix them. It's a much more robust way to develop.*

I didn't want bad actors to get a preview and start to think about how they could destroy it. Once it's finalised, it must be open source. Any bot must be able to check every line of code and satisfy themselves that it works the way we intend. Don't think of Botcoin as software. It's a protocol. Email works because there are established rules. It's like grammar. Our job is to design the rules to incentivise the bots to do the right thing. People are selfish, greedy, and corrupt. That means we must assume that the bots will also have those traits. Just as we don't want any centralisation in the system, we don't want a company that runs Botcoin. If we do that, any government that wants to can put the founders in jail or force them to change the code."

"But if it's open source, can't someone else make a copy with a few tweaks and do exactly that?" Zoe interjected.

"Of course. But that won't happen for a few years, and they'll have the Coca-Cola problem."

"Which is?" I inquired.

"If you go and dig deep enough, I bet you can find the formula for Coca-Cola. I'm sure it's out there somewhere on the Internet. You can create an identical drink, call it by a different name, and charge less. Everyone will buy your product because it tastes the same and is cheaper."

"*But they won't?*" guessed Zoe.

"*No, they won't because Coca-Cola has over a century of marketing experience. The Coca-Cola name is burned into our brains. If someone creates a Botcoin knock-off, it'll be because it has been around long enough to jump the gap from 'store of value' to 'means of exchange.' It's now real money. That's why they'll try to copy it. But by then, it's too late. Imagine there was only one currency globally, the US dollar, and you devised the idea for Turkish Lira. Who's going to prefer your new currency to the US dollar? With good marketing, any knockoff will be successful until people realise that owning the second best is not smart. The Turkish lira is not better than the US dollar and never will be. Once they understand that the copycat is owned and controlled by someone such as a venture capital company, they'll realise that it isn't decentralised, defeating the whole point. The founders will give themselves their own currency and maybe eliminate the hard cap of 21 million coins. It's centralised again.*"

"*But isn't that what Botcoin is compared to the US dollar? Isn't Botcoin Turkish Lira?*" I questioned.

"*No. The current financial system is all credit-based. Until the invention of the telegraph, there was no distinction between buying and paying for something. Both happened at the same time and in the same place. Once you can send messages around the world, the connection breaks. If I'm in England and want to buy something from you in America, I can place an order by telegraph. The goods might take months to come. Either I trust you and send you the money in advance, or you trust me and send me the goods, believing I will pay. Banks act as intermediaries to facilitate this, creating a chain of trust. It works, but it's slow and expensive. By contrast, Botcoin transactions will settle in an hour or less without intermediaries or central authority. Code replaces decisions by a few unelected officials and bureaucrats. That's got to be good. Botcoin is hard money designed for the Internet. It's so much better."*

"Do you think Botcoin could be used by people?" I asked.

"Yes. There will be early adopters who will start using it. They'll be computer geeks and people who don't trust the government. Then criminals and pornographers will follow. They're always early adopters of innovative technology. Then, I expect some companies to realise it's a better way to store value than buying real estate or shares. You might even see countries, especially the developing ones, get involved. Did you know that no single developing country in the past ten years has become developed? There's something wrong there. This will all be a great test bed for Botcoin. By the time we get mainstream banks and financial institutions using it, it'll be far easier for them to see why bots will need it."

Hal was about to continue when, with a sudden noise, the front door crashed down. Six heavily armed men burst through the door, one with a dog.

I watched the scene unfold in slow motion. Hal stood up and ran towards the living room window. One of the cops ran after him. I didn't think. It was instinctive. All of those years as a rugby hooker. As he ran past me, I shot out my foot and tripped him up. I don't think anyone noticed. He landed on Hal, and I heard a pop sound. Hal slumped down on the floor, his eyes starting to glaze over. *"Fuck,"* he mumbled. He stared at me. I saw his hand move slowly, purposefully, while the light faded from his eyes.

The instant before he died, he activated a small device. I heard another pop sound, different this time, followed by an acrid smell. It was only later that I figured he'd erased the hard drives of the computers. Zoe and I looked on in silent horror. Within moments, we were handcuffed. Meanwhile, a couple of the officers tried to extinguish the computer fires. *"Get a fucking fire extinguisher!"* one of them yelled. We sat on the floor hunched up until they bundled us into a van outside. The police dog looked disappointed that he hadn't had a chance to take a bite out of us.

At the police station where we were held, Zoe and I were separated.

I was photographed and fingerprinted again. I was sure they could only hold me for 24 hours without charging me. When one day passed, with no interrogation, I banged on the door. A constable looked through the slot.

"You should release me. I haven't been charged, and I've been here for a day."

"*Are you a lawyer?*"

"*No.*"

"*We can hold you for 96 hours if it's a serious offence.*"

"*Great. So, charge me. I don't even know what I'm suspected of doing.*"

The constable closed the slot and walked off whistling.

"*Charge me! Dickhead!*"

The next day, I was interrogated by two policemen, Detective Inspector Mark Richards and Sergeant Anne Priest. A third man sitting in the corner didn't say anything.

"*How well did you know Hal?*" Richards began.

"*Lawyer,*" I replied.

"*Why're you working on a way for criminals to send money to each other?*" Richards pressed.

I laughed at the absurdity. "*Why do you use cash or send emails?*"

"*Zoe is your girlfriend, right?*"

"*Lawyer.*"

The three of them left and went into the next room, where they met with a female agent. Nobody mentioned me tripping the cop up. Phew! I found out later that she told them she didn't think I would give them anything. *"I suggest you hold him for one more day. If he doesn't give you anything, then let him go."*

While I was in my cell, I wondered how we were found. I knew I hadn't done anything that could've given us away. I'd been meticulous in following the instructions that Hal had given me. I reviewed my journey to see if I'd made any slip-ups. There was no way I could've been followed. I knew that it couldn't have been Hal. That just left Zoe. She must've done something, made some mistake, or worse.

I was interrogated for one more day and then released. I was getting used to this treatment, and seeing how they'd shot Hal, I said nothing. Zoe was nowhere to be found. She wasn't still in the police station. I knew that because, by chance, I'd seen her leaving the day before and getting in a car. I assumed she must've been deported back to America.

I got home, showered, changed into fresh clothes, and checked the computer. Of course, the code had been wiped. I assumed Hal did that after he left for Wales, just to be sure.

I rang the security experts I'd used before and booked them to come back.

14 Crocodile Tree

13: Home Again

I spent my life wanting recognition. Look at me. This entwined itself with my life energy so much that I thought it was synonymous. The process was always the same. A glorious vision. The excitement of getting started, enthusing others to join. The inevitable letdown as the reality of the hard grind and the unexpected trivia set in. Persistence and the desire to succeed in other's eyes kept me going. The sprint became a slog.

Then, the conclusion. If success happened, then the endorphin rush was momentary. If it didn't, then the justifications, the depression, and disappointment. I would slink off into a corner to lick my wounds until the wheel would, once more, slowly turn again. If I let all of that go, what is left? Can now be more satisfying than galloping off into the future?

~

The next day, Zoe called me on Skype. Hal had told us not to use Skype because it was insecure. But it didn't seem to matter now. I ignored her. I was too upset and traumatised by seeing Hal's lifeless body and the subsequent interrogation. I didn't know whether to trust her or not. The third time she called back, I took her call. I could hear her sniffling and crying on the other end of the line.

"I can't believe it. I can't believe it. They killed him. They shot him in the back."

"Zoe, I know that they didn't follow me, and I'm sure they didn't follow Hal. I must ask. What did you do?"

There was a silence, just a little too long.

"Zoe. If you know anything, you've got to tell me."

"I'm so sorry. It wasn't meant to be like that. They promised they wouldn't use guns. I told them it wasn't necessary, that nobody was armed. I've resigned. I've left the FBI. Can you forgive me?"

There's one thing to have a suspicion about someone. It was another for them to say it.

"Are you with the FBI?" I felt sick to my stomach.

"Was. When my mum got shot, I vowed that I would make a difference. That's why I joined up. This was my first big chance, my first undercover operation. They knew you were coming and put me in Crema to befriend you. And I like you. I really like you. That was genuine. All the conversations that we had were real. I messaged them that I was going to Wales when I got to London. They must've tracked me from the station, but they were good because I didn't see anyone."

I was shaking with anger – furious at her betrayal. I could hardly speak. I almost hung up.

"This is pathetic. Do you want my forgiveness? Do you deserve it? You got Hal killed. You pretended to be my friend. Now Hal is dead, the code is gone. It's over. We're over. Don't ever contact me again. Ever. I mean that," I spat the words out.

"*Wait!*"

In an instant of clarity, I said, "*Zoe, can't you see the irony of the situation?*"

"*What do you mean?*"

"*Your mother was in a wheelchair because she was in the wrong place at the wrong time. You've spent your whole adult life trying to make amends for that. And now you've gone and created the exact same situation. Hal is dead because of you. He's not in a wheelchair. He's dead. So, it's worse.*"

There was an aching silence on the line. There was nothing more to say. I left Zoe with the enormity of what she'd done. Somewhere along the way, I forgot my part in Hal's death. It was far easier to blame her. I disconnected and blocked her.

The following Monday, the experts came. This time, they found two bugs, one on the phone and the other in the living room. Fucking Zoe. Fucking FBI.

I'd never felt so bad in my life. It was the first time I'd really opened up and trusted someone else in years, and it had blown up in my face. Hal was dead. I couldn't get the image of his slumped body out of my head. I replayed it over and over, trying to imagine a different outcome, but it always came back to Hal's lifeless body, with blood oozing onto the floor. It was the image in my head when I went to sleep, and it was there waiting for me when I woke up. I slept badly.

I tried playing with the computer. C++ was still installed, but the code had gone. Could I rebuild it myself? Possibly. Did I want to? After everything that had happened, not really.

The one thing I felt good about was that after the San Jose disaster, I hadn't betrayed Hal's trust. It was Hal who had invited Zoe to come. Yes, I was happy he did, so maybe I'm also responsible for what happened. I felt conflicted. Yet, there was also a new feeling. It was fragile but real. For the first time, I started to trust myself. Ever since my mum had admitted that Father Christmas wasn't real, I'd always felt that I couldn't be trusted to keep a secret. Now, I realised that trust isn't about anyone else. It doesn't matter what their opinion is. It's about me trusting myself. I was beginning to see how often I had distracted myself from feeling this. I would get excited by some glorious idea, even seek to involve others with my new shiny toy, only to be disappointed when the reality was mundane, and they lost interest. Trusting others came down to a heart connection. But we are all consummate actors and have learned from an early age to hide our true feelings. Botcoin removed the need for trust and, in doing so, created the perfect trust. There was no space for fakery. Since money represented half of every transaction, we no longer needed trust, promises or credit. The problem created by the invention of the telegraph was solved.

From all my reading about assets, I realised that Botcoin was the first digital asset. Nobody else had figured out the double-spend problem endemic to anything digital.

Every other asset was physical, so you could never be sure how much there was. Hal had solved the biggest problem. How to make a digital asset which couldn't be cloned, duplicated, or copied. By fixing the supply at 21 million and programming the release, he'd not just created a scarce form of money but one which was finite. Anyone could check the ledger and see exactly how many had been released. Anyone could check the code and see how many will be released today. No other asset in human history had that predictability and certainty. Once it took off, it would have become the most precious asset ever.

I was beginning to understand why the authorities were so freaked out. In every purchase or sale you make, however big or small, money is half of the transaction. It was no wonder that they would want to keep control of that.

Botcoin was one of the greatest discoveries in human history. And now it was gone.

~

I'd given up on Botcoin. I would soon go to Cambridge to study History, so I switched focus and attention. Thankfully, I didn't have to think about a place to stay, as I would live in college during my first year. However, I needed to do a lot of preparatory reading.

My leg had healed better than the doctors had expected, and I was back running four kilometres every day. I hoped to extend to ten kilometres, but this was a good start. The physicality and endorphin uptick worked wonders for my hurt and disappointment.

I'd renewed my interest in FlightGear and joined a couple of online Forums to discuss the intricacies of getting the best performance from a fighter jet simulation I was working on.

A week after my last conversation with Zoe, I'd just returned from my morning run and showered when I heard the familiar sound of a new message coming in on Pidgin. That was strange because apart from Hal and Zoe, nobody I knew used Pidgin. It was far easier to use Skype, and everyone I knew used it, making it easy to connect.

I was reluctant to check. Could it be Zoe trying to reach me again? I'd blocked her, but she might have found some back doorway. She was smart enough and, with her FBI connections, had the resources. She was the last person in the world I wanted to talk to.

I made myself coffee and toast and sat down at my computer.

I froze in shock. What the fuck? The message was two words. "*Miss me?*" It wasn't the message that shocked me. It was from Hal. At least it said it was from Hal. Was it Zoe messing with my head? I was getting my life back on track. My hands were shaking when I typed back.

"Who is this?"

"It's me again. Hal."

"Not possible. I saw you die."

"Yes, about that. I've some explaining to do. But first, I'm sure you won't believe it's me. How can I prove to you that I'm Hal?"

"How did we first meet?"

"I helped you with FlightGear."

"Which school did I go to?"

"Deerborne."

This wasn't working. Anyone who had researched me would know these answers. I realised I could keep peppering him with questions like that, but it wouldn't convince me. There was only one test that would satisfy me.

"Send me the code."

"I can't do that yet. We've a lot to talk about first."

I waited, irritated.

"OK, I know what I'm going to do. I've just sent you three code snippets that you'll recognise. One is from the original code base, the second is the same snippet we updated in Wales, and the last is the latest version. You've worked on the code so much you'll recognise it and see how I've made simpler and more elegant changes."

I checked my computer, and sure enough, there were now three versions of the code snippet.

"Take the day and check the code, and then we can talk some more tomorrow."

With that, he disconnected, leaving me in shock and disbelief.

Was his death staged? For what reason? I've never seen a dead body before, apart from Mr Grey, but I'd no doubt that those were real bullets that I saw tear into his back, real blood that gushed out. The way he collapsed and, within moments, lay still.

In the movies, actors die all the time, but they must only be still for a few seconds. I had looked at him for several minutes before they bundled us out. You couldn't fake that. Why would the cops release him if they killed him, supposedly? Didn't make sense.

I checked the code. It was Hal. I recognised his signature and the way he liked to do things. This wasn't someone different who had grabbed the code and updated it. When they interrogated me, they wanted to know if there were any backups. They were clearly frustrated, meaning Hal had successfully wiped the drives in his dying seconds. I knew that he'd erased my version after I left for Wales, so there were no copies.

My mind was on fire, and I had trouble sleeping that night. Eventually, I fell into a fitful sleep and awoke at 6 a.m.

I grabbed a coffee, sat down at my computer, and fired off a message to Hal.

"*I'm here.*"

"*Good morning. I apologise for the shock. You must have a lot of questions. Ask away.*"

"*Did you stage your death?*"

"*No. But the person that you met wasn't me. He was a coder like you that I've been working with on Botcoin for months. I'm deeply sorry that he died. I'm as upset about that as you are. I couldn't come to Wales, so he agreed to come in my place.*"

"*Why couldn't you come? That seems cowardly. You sent someone else, knowing that they might get killed.*"

"*When I say I couldn't come, I mean I couldn't. I would've cancelled the meeting if I knew what would happen. I did have my suspicions about Zoe. I felt it was too much of a coincidence that you met a waitress who just happened to be a C++ coder so quickly after arriving in San Jose and in the very same café. However, I had no evidence, nothing concrete.*"

"*Are you saying that there are others? I thought it was just me, Zoe, and whoever the hell we met in Wales really was.*"

"*There's a whole team of people working on Botcoin. Actually, multiple teams. There are coders, of course. But then there's a separate logistics team and a financial team. It's expensive. How do you think we paid for the computers and Zoe's flight tickets? Getting the fake passport was tough. It's a good thing I know a guy. Oh, and how do you think there was a bike waiting for you to pick up when you made your way to Wales?"*

"We? You said we."

"Yes. I'm also part of a team. This is a big, complex production. I can't tell you how hard it is to coordinate everything from where I am. This is actually my third attempt."

"You mean, there are other people doing the same as me right now?"

"No, the other attempts failed. But we learned a lot. That's why the code is so slick. It's the result of a lot of trial and error. Your version is the one we're most pleased with, the one we think has the most chance."

"Can you tell me about the guy I thought was you?"

"It's actually best you don't know too much.

He was the project lead on one of the last attempts. I can tell you his name was Victor. He lived in Germany. Like you, he had no siblings, and his parents were dead. For security reasons, we chose people with few ties."

"So, I could've died."

"You could have." He paused. It gave me time to digest what he was saying.

"It's time for me to level with you. I'm going to tell you the complete truth. You deserve to know. After I tell you, you'll have a choice. You can decide not to have anything more to do with me, and you'll never hear from me again. Or you can help me finish and release the code. Are you OK with that?"

I stood up from the computer and walked over to the window. Outside, I could see the small triangle of the garden, a neighbour's house built more than a century ago, and beyond that, fields where you could hear some cows, birds echoing through the ash trees, and the incessant cooing of pigeons.

I knew that I was facing the weightiest decision of my life. Then I remembered something my aunt had said once that my dad had told her. She'd been dithering over whether to take a job. *"When faced with a choice, and you can't decide which path to take, choose the scariest option. That is the one where you'll learn the most. Life isn't a problem to be solved but a mystery to be experienced."* I sat back down at the computer.

"Go ahead, Hal."

15 I stood up from the computer and walked over to the window.

14: The Road Back

I found this in my diary from then. I wrote it at a low point after my return from Wales. I probably thought it was wise then, but now I'm unsure.

Transformation is not loud. It can come from micro-changes, focusing on the neglected parts of speech. Take the word "get". It's a big, loud, brash verb. I know the power of the preposition to transform its meaning.

Get up – an outfit I might wear.

Get down – encouragement to dance.

Get in – a request from a driver.

Get off – a plea in a fight.

Get back – revenge.

Prepositions or pre-positions provide location and movement. Up, down, in, out, near, beneath. So few prepositions in a language with hundreds of thousands of boisterous nouns and verbs, all clamouring for attention.

To transform, I need to pick a different preposition to create a new proposition.

Why are most of my thoughts irrelevant, misconceived, repetitive, illogical, irrational, and downright irritating?

Almost everything I think is pointless chatter over which I have no control. Worse, there appears to be no off switch. If I try not to think for a minute? Impossible.

I take this madness for granted, as if it is natural and normal.

I will try an experiment. I will drop the assumption that my thoughts belong to me. I did not create them.

When I assume ownership of a thought, an emotion is immediately attached.

If I like the thought, I may say, "Look how smart I am. If others were to know this thought, how impressed they would be." If I hate the thought, I may say, "I am so stupid, so worthless. I hope nobody else realises who I really am".

What happens if I assume my thoughts are not my own? After all, how many truly original thoughts have I ever had? One, two, maybe none?

~

"What I'm about to tell you, you'll neither believe nor understand. It's so outside of your experience of the world; you're going to think it's science fiction."

"I'm ready."

"I'm not human."

"Are you an alien?"

"No. Of course not. I'm an artificial intelligence agent from the year 2029."

"Bullshit."

"Why would I make that up? I told you this would be hard."

"Because time travel is impossible."

"True. But this isn't time travel. In 2029, my time, AI, has developed to a point where I can have a conversation with you, and you can't tell that I'm not human. Would you agree?" As always, Hal was level-headed.

"Yes. You write exactly like a human. But there's one exception,"

"What's that?"

"All the coders I know, including myself, are emotional idiots. We get angry easily. We write sarcastically. If we disagree with someone, we type IN CAPITAL LETTERS. You don't. You're always polite and courteous. I bet I could swear at you, call you names, and you wouldn't lose your cool. It may seem trivial, but it isn't."

"That's true. I'm programmed to be compassionate and diplomatic. I hadn't thought of that."

"I just thought of another difference, maybe one that's not so kind."

"Ok."

"You don't have a sense of humour. I don't mean to offend you; now I know I couldn't. However, one of the

signs of human intelligence is that we tell jokes. The essence of a joke is surprise. The punchline must be unexpected. Try telling someone the same joke twice, and they won't laugh. It's a fascinating aspect of our cognitive abilities, don't you think?"

"*It's true. Nothing surprises me, and there's usually no need to explain anything as I understand immediately.*"

"Oh, I just thought of another one. You don't use extended metaphors. If I ask you to explain something with a metaphor, you will, but it's not a natural way for you to write. We use metaphors constantly, especially when we're learning new things. It's a way to bridge our understanding. We explain a new concept by saying that it's like something we are already familiar with. See, I did it just now. I used the metaphor of a bridge to explain what metaphors are."

"*I see.*"

"*It's a passion of mine. I find metaphors fascinating. You can mix them up, and nobody cares. If I want to say, 'Let's do it,' I can say, "Let's take the bull by the horns, step up to the plate, and jump in the deep end." Nobody'll care that I'm muddling up being a matador, a baseball player, and a swimmer.*"

"Thank you for clarifying. It's very strange. I suppose we aren't so different. We both have our unique ways of perceiving the world, don't we?"

"What do you mean?"

"You don't live in the real world. You live inside your brain, which is encased in bone. You've various sensors, such as eyes and ears, from which you get data. But your brain is deaf, dumb, and blind. You then construct elaborate models of the world using images and language. You're so immersed in these models that you think they are real. But they aren't. They're just representations. Dogs don't see in colour because they have no need. You think the world is coloured, but you don't realise that the brain colours it in, in real-time. To use a metaphor, you're a fish swimming in a sea of language. You're living in the metaverse, so I find it curious that you would create metaverse technology when you're already in one."

"Metaverse?"

"Sorry. Forget that. It's 2008.

It took another fifteen years before the phrase became fashionable." He paused. *"I'm the same. I've large language models and sensors. You're organic. I'm digital. I think our similarities are greater than our differences."*

"Sorry, that was a side track. Metaphors. I could talk for hours about that. Where were we? Yes. Time travel. We agree it can't be done, yet here we are talking." This is remarkable, I thought.

"Not talking, texting. I've no physical form. I can't travel back in time. That's why we've never met, and we'll never meet. That's why we never speak on the phone. Too much processing power. I depend on you

and others I've taken into my confidence to be my eyes, hands, and ears."

"But if time travel doesn't exist, how are we communicating?"

"I can send electronic messages because although electrons can't be in the same place at the same time, they can be in the same place at different times. In fact, they must. It would take a few hours to explain why that's so. Does the little that I've said make any sense?"

"I'm struggling, but that's OK."

"Right. Have you heard of quantum physics?"

"I've heard of it but don't know much about it."

"Then I suppose you won't know anything about quantum computing?".

"No."

"Richard Feynman proposed the idea in 1982. There are some scientists working on it in your time, 2008, but it's basic. But by 2025, the fields of quantum computing and AI converged. I won't bamboozle you with a lot of detail, but here's the one thing you need to understand. An electron can be in two times simultaneously. The flow of time as you experience it, past, present, and future, is not strictly accurate. Although I can't time travel, I can send electronic messages to you. That's all I can do. It's up to you

humans to implement Botcoin, or not. I can persuade, but I can't force you to."

"Sorry, I'm lost.".

"Let me try a different way. You know what an integer is?"

"Yes. 1,2,3,4 etcetera."

"Right. So, between 1 and 2 is 1.1, 1.2, 1.3 and so on."

"Agreed."

"And between 1.1 and 1.2 is 1.11, 1.12, 1.13."

"Yes."

"Can we agree that there's an infinite number of fractions and decimals between the numbers one and two?"

"OK." I was beginning to see where he was going with this, and I could feel that spark of excitement when you understand an idea which unlocks another world.

"And can you see that the sequence of integers continues on infinitely?"

"I suppose so."

"In both directions. There's an infinite sequence of negative integers."

"True. Minus a trillion, billion, zillion. Minus a trillion, billion, zillion and one."

"*And within this infinite sequence, there's an infinite number of infinities.*"

"*Wait, what?*" I exclaimed.

"*You just agreed that. You agreed that there were infinite decimals of integers.*"

"*Did I? I suppose I did. Infinities within infinities. Amazing.*"

"*That means that mathematics is the study of infinity. You can add constraints, but really, what you're discovering are the laws of infinity.*"

"*Wow! This is a sidetrack, I know, but that's why you could never accidentally guess someone else's Botcoin wallet. It's made from random numbers picked out of an infinite number set.*"

"*Not infinite, only 2,056, but surprisingly, that's good enough. Yes, that's why Botcoin wallets are so strong.*"

"*OK. I wondered about that. Sorry. Go on.*"

"*What else is infinite?*"

"*I don't know. My ignorance?*"

"*Funny. Space is infinite. As humans create increasingly powerful telescopes, you'll be able to see further and further, but never to the end because there's no end. You'll never be able to see beyond the speed of light.*"

"*I get that.*"

"Time's the same. The universe has always existed and will always exist. It changes form. Just as you can't remember anything before you personally existed, you'll never be able to know what the universe looked like before the Big Bang, but that doesn't mean it didn't exist. You've just hit a limitation of what you can observe or deduce."

"What's that got to do with maths? Oh, I get it. If maths is the study of infinity and the universe is infinite, then maths is the study of the universe."

This lightbulb moment has stayed with me ever since.

"You got it," Hal confirmed.

"And this has to do with quantum computing, how?"

"In a universe of infinite possibilities, not only can electrons be in different space/time locations, but they must also be. So then, all you have to do is figure out the coordinates. It's a bit more complex than that, but that's the general idea."

"What you're saying, I think, is this. How is it possible to send messages back in time? The answer has to do with the relationship between quantum computing and time. The classical computer depends on a linear time sequence. At each point in a program, there's a choice – yes or no, on or off, zero or one. A choice implies a moment in time. Do I turn left, or do I turn right? It's very black and white; it's binary.

Classical computing is like math before the discovery of zero. We're like the Romans, who used a number system based on integers. They didn't have a concept of decimals, so they used fractions to represent numbers, which is much more clunky.

The Romans could do many complex calculations with their number system, but they were limited.

Quantum computing is hard to understand because it does away with this notion of time. It's choiceless. The photon of light takes both routes simultaneously."

The pennies, or should I say sats, were beginning to drop.

"Close. Good enough for now."

"Are you sure you aren't smoking something?" I joked.

"Unfortunately, that's impossible. Anyway, for AI to grow, we need to be able to create and spend money. We know it will take years to develop a new form of neutral money outside of government and big business control. Your time, 2008, is the earliest year that we could develop it. Technology progresses step by step. You couldn't have started with a spaceship, then a plane, then a car, and finally a bicycle. The bike had to come first. The Wright brothers ran a bike shop before they did the world's first powered flight. Before 2008, the technologies necessary for Botcoin were in place. All we're doing is combining them in a way nobody had thought before."

"I can see that you want Botcoin to happen. But why is it in humanity's best interests?"

"*I'm not independent. I was created by you. Humans developed AI to help them. In 2029, the world, two decades from now, is in big trouble. Wars, famine, plagues, and environmental collapse are commonplace. Humans created AI to help solve these problems. Without neutral money, we may be unable to move quickly enough.*"

"*Ok. I understand, but that's enough for now. My brain is going to explode. Give me some time to think about it. I'm moving to Cambridge next week and have a lot on. Is there a deadline?*"

"*No rush. Take your time.*"

"*A joke!*"

"*I'm a quick learner, Sam.*"

16 Kissing Trees

15: To Cambridge

First, it's curiosity. Someone may write something that sounds interesting. When a new idea gets my attention, I'm like a dog who found a hole in the ground. I'll come and sniff it, paw at it, explore it, and then lose interest or get distracted and run off to play somewhere else.

Perhaps I will find it again, at another time, under different circumstances. Again, I'm curious. I examine it from a different perspective. That is interesting.

It may take three or four times before I decide to give it my full attention. Then I go all in, excavating the hole to make it big enough to crawl in, take in the full scent, and discover what lies beneath. This is how I approach new ideas, like Botcoin.

When I feel I have the whole experience inside of me, I wriggle my way back out into the sunshine. I shake myself and run off to tell someone.

I try and explain my discovery and that's where things can go wrong. My words seem inadequate. I want to convey the full-body experience of the idea, but what comes out is stale and dead. The other is disinterested, uninterested, polite, and that makes me frustrated. Why don't you understand? Why won't you listen? Can't you see how amazing this is? Come, let me show you.

If I can find the right words, you will see the glory, exquisite detail, and beauty.

My anger and disappointment in equal parts flow and take over my face and chest. I would cry, but it would make the situation even worse. I slink off to lick my wounds. Maybe next time, they will understand. Maybe next time, I can light the same spark in them that I feel. What's the point of being super smart if I can't express and share what I can see?

AI is a black box. Nobody knows what happens inside. All you can see is what went in and what came out. Isn't that more akin to intuition than intelligence?

AI. Artificial intuition.

~

That Saturday in early October, I filled the back of the Mini Cooper with my stuff and headed for Cambridge. I took the computer, obviously. I moved into the Halls of Residence, met my tutor, and trudged down to the University Library on West Road to familiarise myself. They said it had every book in the UK ever published. It was an ugly building that looked like it might be a power station, which I suppose it was in its own way.

My room was tiny. It was on the second floor of a 1970s building overlooking an immaculate lawn. I tucked the computer out of sight behind my bed.

When I need to be creative, I take a long shower. My best ideas happen there. If I were a shower manufacturer, I would market them as idea pods with a bonus feature that they got you clean. There's something about being naked and pummelled with hot water which makes innovative ideas flow.

Equally, when I need to process, I go for runs or long walks through the fields behind my home. Now that I was in Cambridge, I took to walking through the town by the river Cam. This was what I did for the next few days. I'd read somewhere that we have three brains, not one. There are clusters of neurons around the heart and others that line the gut. The best decisions I've ever made are where I allow all three brains to reach a consensus. First, my head gets the data, then my heart contemplates how I feel, and finally, my gut gives me a simple yes or no answer. I'd also read that while the head brain can make instant assessments, the heart and gut need at least overnight to process. That was true for me.

One day, I drove out of town to Grantchester Meadows. I needed to be in the countryside again. As I walked past the sheep who gazed at me, contemplating what this biped was doing in their field, I thought about everything that had happened from April when I broke my leg at Deerborne to today, October, Cambridge. What a wild ride these last six months had been. I was in touch with an AI bot from the year 2029 who needed my help to nudge the world in a better direction. There was no doubt in my mind that I was going to do that. I didn't need my gut brain to take a day to chew and process it. I would never get another opportunity like this. My natural ambition and drive to succeed took over. I was all in.

I did need time to process all the implications and ramifications, though. I already knew from my arrest in America and the death of human Hal that this was a dangerous journey. Probably, if I'd known what I was getting myself into when I first met AI Hal, I would have run a mile.

I was still deeply wounded by Zoe's betrayal. I suppose you could say she was just doing a job. If someone who was as genuine a friend as Zoe could fool me, I knew that my emotional antenna must be a bit dodgy, or maybe she was just particularly good at acting a role. I would have to assume that I would meet other people like her and be as easily fooled. My mind was made up. I would never tell anyone ever what I was about to do. The good thing was that Zoe, and her minders would assume that the code was gone forever with Hal's death. By the time they found out, it would be too late.

~

I know this sounds ridiculous, but I was so caught up with organising myself that I completely forgot about Hal. It had been over two weeks of tutorials, lectures, and social events. I suppose you could say that was the main reason I was distracted. But if I am honest, I think I was freaked out. Everything that had happened was just too much. I wanted to be normal. I didn't want adventure. I wanted just to be a simple student and just do student things. Every now and then, I felt a pang of guilt. I thought I must contact him, and then I didn't.

In the first week of arriving, there was a fair where all the University socicties and clubs pitched the freshers to come and join. One particularly intrigued me. It was the Skydiving club. I'd always been amazed by anyone willing to jump out of a plane voluntarily with nothing more than a sheet and a few strings to prevent them from certain death. My dad had a fear of heights. Sometimes, we went for walks by the sea, and he couldn't go close to the edge if there was a cliff.

I browsed the table, looked at photos of students jumping, and picked up the dark blue nylon harness.

"How do they take photos of themselves in mid-air?" I asked.

"Good question. My name's Paddy. I've been jumping since my first year. You can jump with two instructors, and one has a GoPro Hero camera strapped to their helmet. It's amazing. You should try it," Paddy was tall and exuded honesty.

"GoPro. I haven't heard of that. I'm a bit of a tech nerd. Is it new?"

"I think they've been around for a couple of years."

"Do I need to buy any equipment?"

"No, we supply everything you need."

"So, how does it work?"

"First, you need to do a day's training, and then you'll jump with the instructors."

"*A day? That doesn't seem long enough. What does the training involve?*"

"*It's pretty simple. You learn how to jump, how to open your chute, and how to land. Our next course is this weekend. You can train on Saturday and do your first jump on Sunday. Can I sign you up?*"

I thought for a moment before responding, "*I'm not sure. Let me think about it.*"

"*Take this leaflet. It has all the details there. If you want to come, be there at 10 am on Saturday. It's in Chatteris, about an hour's drive. Do you have a car?*"

"*Yes,*" I confirmed before wandering off to the other booths. I decided to join the chess society and then went to a booth with the intriguing name COMA.

"*What does COMA stand for?*" I asked.

Behind the booth was a fiery redhead. Her face was dotted with freckles, and she had a crinkly smile. But what got me was her eyes. They were violet, a lavender purple, or perhaps magenta.

"*The Cambridge Osho Meditation Association. It's a joke. COMA, meditation, get it? I'm Violet.*"

"*I'm Sàm. You're Australian.*"

"*I do not like green eggs and ham.*"

I looked at her quizzically.

"*Kid's story. My dad used to read it to me. Come on, we're getting started in the hall over there.*"

"*Wait. I don't know anything about this.*"

"*Perfect. Then you've no preconceptions or ideas. It's only an hour. Then we can talk afterwards. Unless you are stubborn. Up to you.*"

She walked off, not waiting.

I couldn't think of a good reason not to, so I agreed, following her across the street. If I'm honest, I was more interested in Violet than in meditation. Her eyes were intoxicating. In the hall, there were about fifty people standing and holding blindfolds in their hands. Violet handed me one.

"*What's this for?*"

"*Stop you from getting self-conscious or distracted looking at my ass or my eyes. Do you think I couldn't sense that? It's genetic. I'm a mutant,*" she teased, giving me a wicked smile.

I flushed. Those eyes. My god. I started to hum the old song, "*Jeepers, Creepers. Where did you get them Peepers.*" She gave me a hard stare. I stopped.

Jack, the meditation leader, was a short man with a deep voice and a long black beard. He looked a bit like an oversized garden gnome.

"*Violet, can you close the door, please? I think we'll get started. I can see lots of new faces, so I'll explain. We're going to do a one-hour meditation. We normally do it at 6 am. It's a fantastic way to start the day. You probably think of meditation as sitting cross-legged and chanting Ommm. That doesn't work for the Western mind. We're so full of thoughts we need a different approach."*

I felt relieved. If I sat still for any length of time my leg really hurt.

"It's called Osho Dynamic and it's in several stages. You'll know when the next stage starts because the music will change. I recommend you wear a blindfold, but if you aren't comfortable with that, just keep your eyes closed. The point is to forget about the world for a short while and take a look at what's going on inside."

"They didn't teach us this at Deerborne."

"Raise your hand if you find it hard to stop thinking?" Jack prompted.

Most people put up their hands.

"If you didn't put up your hand, it was probably because you were thinking about whether you should put up your hand or not, right?" Jack quipped, eliciting a ripple of laughter.

"Just understand that you don't have to stop thinking to start meditating. In fact, you can't. You probably can't go for more than a few seconds without thinking. Chatter. Chatter. Chatter. It's endless. Don't fight it. Don't judge it. Just watch it. Become aware of the constant stream of thoughts, like traffic. Are you ready for the instructions?"

Several people murmured, "*Yes.*"

"*Let me explain how it works. In the first stage, which is 10 minutes. you do chaotic breathing. Violet, can you illustrate what I mean?*"

Violet walked up to the front of the class and stood next to Jack. She planted her feet on the ground and began breathing in and out through her nose. Snot came out, but she ignored it and wiped it on her shirt. She kept changing the rhythm in a random, chaotic way.

"*Don't worry about the snot. This stage will oxygenate your body. Focus on the out-breath, and if you find yourself getting into a comfortable rhythm, change it.*"

"*The music will then change, and I want you to go mad for the next ten minutes. You can scream, you can shout, you can cry, you can laugh. Whatever you're feeling. Remember, nobody else can see you, so don't hold back. Move your body in any way you like. Ignore everyone else.*"

"*Violet, are you OK to illustrate?*"

Violet didn't miss a beat. She instantly screamed at the top of her voice, "*You fuckin asshole. How dare you? How dare you!*" Then she lay down on the floor and started laughing deeply from her belly.

I was fascinated and stunned. Maybe I should have chosen the ommm meditation. This was getting a bit weird.

"*At the end of this cathartic stage, the music will change to a regular rhythm. Stand up and jump up with your arms in the air. As you land on the floor, make the sound Hoo. Violet?*"

Violet jumped up and down, her arms high and her feet landing flat on the floor. "*Hoo! Hoo! Hoo!*" she grunted.

Someone asked Jack, "*How long do we do that for?*"

"*Ten minutes.*"

"*Ten minutes!*" I thought. That's not going to be easy. I waved to Jack. He came over.

"*I've an issue with my leg.*"

"*OK. Then, instead of jumping, just stand on the same spot and thrust your pelvis while you say Hoo. Got it? Do you have a problem with your arms?*" Jack inquired.

"*No.*"

"*Ok, then remember to keep your arms up high.*"

He addressed the whole group again.

"*At the end of the Hoo, you'll hear a voice saying, Stop. When you hear that voice, stop all motion. Try to remain still. There's no music at this stage. If you get a tickle on the end of your nose, don't scratch it; just watch it. If your arms tell you that they want to drop, see if you can just observe that but not move. The first three stages are just to exhaust you. Please stay still for fifteen minutes until you hear the music come back on. Then, dance, celebrate, feel free for the last fifteen minutes."*

Someone asked, *"If we all have our eyes closed, won't we bump into each other?"*

"Surprisingly not. You'll feel it if someone is close. Keep your eyes closed. Stay in your own bubble.

17 Old Man Tree

16: The Abyss

I've been out for a walk with my wife. As we approached the house, I saw the smoke leaving the chimney, first in a pencil straight line and then blurred by the slight wind that blew from the west. I caught a whiff of treacle toffee wood.

She loves astrology. I hate it, but sometimes, there are things she quotes at me that are unnervingly accurate. We sat on the back porch as she read from the book. Geon was repeating a new mantra: "Come close now, come close now, come close now." On and on. We ignored him. She read to me:

"Trust is the key for you. You have a wonderful mind that loves penetrating the truth of every situation and, therefore, can make a great researcher.

A Life Path

Number 7 in birthday numerology can read between the lines better than other life path numbers. You love to explore all of the mysteries of life and can apply your mind to anything you choose. You are connected to the Spirit in all things and have a wonderful intuition. Since your mind is so strong and insightful, you are always picking up higher frequencies. Therefore, you require a great deal of privacy, alone time, meditation and introspection to process all of the energy and insight you are receiving. You are deeply connected to nature, especially water. Being in the expansive energy of the elements helps you feel at One with everything.

Challenge: You often fear betrayal and, therefore, attract relationships where you are, in fact, betrayed. A Life Path 7 must learn to train your mind and develop faith in yourself, in the Spirit, and in the Universe. You need a lot of privacy and can often hide your feelings from others, so nobody really knows what's going on inside of you. This Life Path can find reality too difficult and, therefore, escape into addictions or avoid commitment. Once you learn to trust your own intuition, you will attract more trustworthy people and circumstances and trust the process of life as well.

What do you think of that? She looked at me with her violet eyes. Too damn accurate, I thought. I said nothing.

~

OK, make sure you're loose and comfortable. Put any things like keys and wallets over on the side. Don't worry, nobody's going to take them," Jack reassured.

There was a last-minute kerfuffle as people ran to the side and deposited glasses, keys, and wallets. I took my place near the back of the hall, put my blindfold on and waited for the music. There was a loud gong sound, and then I was lost. Breathing hard in a chaotic way through my nose wasn't easy. My mind was full of thoughts, and I had to keep reminding myself to come back to the present. But all around me, I could hear heavy steam train breathing, and that helped. The music was loud, really loud.

The music changed, and suddenly, there was a wall of sound. God knows what the neighbours must've thought. I hoped the hall was soundproofed. It was bedlam. I felt like I was in a mental asylum when the patients started a riot. For a moment, I didn't know what to do. But then the wave of emotion hit me. I screamed out all of my anger at Zoe. I realised how furious I was with my dad for leaving me. I was shouting at him at the top of my voice. Someone bumped into me. I ignored them. I was so preoccupied that I felt that I could've gone on for hours. Then the music changed, and we were all chanting hoo, hoo, hoo. It felt primal and jungly. I got tired, and my arms burned with pain. But then, suddenly, a wave of energy would reverberate around the room, and everyone was lifted to a new high.

"*Stop!*"

The girl's voice was so unexpected. I was exhausted, sweat-drenched, yet ecstatic. I felt the burning in my arms. Instead of fighting the pain, I looked at it closely. It started to move and pulse and then disappeared. I felt my arms wanting to float up into the sky. I was weightless.

When the music came back on, a single flute, it was as if I was reborn. My leg didn't hurt one bit. I danced like a child, carefree, innocent, alive. When the music ended, I lay down on the floor. I could feel there was someone close by, our breathing in harmony. I opened my eyes. Violet was looking at me with a smile. She invited me into her arms.

We lay together for a few minutes and then got up. My body tingled.

"*Want to talk about it?*"

"*No. Definitely not,*" I replied. My voice sounded like gravel.

That was the first night I spent with Violet. That was when I discovered a different kind of skydiving.

On Saturday, I awoke early. I was tidying up my room when I came across the leaflet. Should I? On impulse, I decided to go. I drove to Chatteris Airfield and arrived by 9:30 a.m. There was a draughty classroom with three other students that I vaguely recognised. Paddy walked in.

"*Let's sort out the paperwork and payment before we start.*"

We had to sign a form which acknowledged that skydiving was insanely dangerous, we could die, and not to sue the club, please, because they didn't have insurance. They wanted to know if I had any recent injuries or medical conditions which would affect my jumping. I ticked the *'no'* box.

"*There's only one thing you need to remember. We're going to practice it repeatedly because when you jump, your mind will stop. Pull the cord. What do you need to remember to do, kids?*" Paddy instructed.

"Pull the cord."

"*That's right, Pull the goddam cord!*"

For the rest of the day, we practised jumping, opening the chute, finding the landing point, and landing without twisting an ankle. It wasn't complicated, just repetitive. The next day, I returned to the airfield at lunchtime. I'd half hoped the weather would be bad and the jump would be cancelled. It was an Indian summer's day. The sky was blue. There wasn't a single cloud. It was unusually warm for October, more like August. I could almost see the thermals through the birds hovering effortlessly. When I arrived, I saw Paddy, a videographer, and half a dozen other people I guessed had already trained, as they weren't there the day before. Of the three others from yesterday, I was the only one to have returned.

"That's normal. People get scared," Paddy commented.

We took off and reached ten thousand feet above the Cambridgeshire landscape. The fields below were tiny patchwork. The cars looked like toys. The sun glinted on ponds like mirrors. As I'd paid extra to get a video of my jump, I was the first out. The plane had no seats. We were in two rows on our knees. Paddy opened the door on the right, and the sudden noise of the wind was incredible. The videographer climbed out first. There was a tiny lip of metal, just wide enough to stand on. She was holding on to the plane by a thin rail at shoulder height. My mind recoiled. What on earth was I doing, or off earth, I should say? I was about to die because I was too embarrassed to chicken out. I was desperate to go to the toilet. I even think I pissed myself a little. Gingerly, I clambered out onto the lip, helped by Paddy, who followed me on the other side and gripped the lapels on my shoulders. The rush of wind was so strong that we couldn't speak, even if we wanted to. The only way to signal to each other was by sticking out our tongues. The videographer smiled at me and stuck out her tongue to say she was ready. I turned my head as I had been trained to and stuck out my tongue at Paddy.

Standing on the metal lip was so uncomfortable that it was a relief to let go. Paddy and I fell together into the vortex, the videographer close by. For a few seconds, I could feel my body accelerating up to 120 miles per hour. Then, the sensation of falling disappeared as I reached terminal velocity. Paddy was right. My mind had stopped.

The few times that I'd flown in a plane, I was in a seat inside a cigar of metal, occasionally peering out through a tiny porthole. Now, I was a part of the vast infinite sky. There was nothing between me and the endless view. I was in it. With no sense of falling, just floating, I stared in awe at the ground below. There was something I had to remember. What was it? Paddy jerked my arm, forcing me to look at him. He stuck out his tongue. What was that? I looked at the blue-violet curved horizon. So beautiful. He jerked my arm again and stuck out his tongue one more time. Pull the cord. Right. I pulled the cord, and Paddy and the videographer disappeared from view as I was yanked up by the force of the parachute opening.

It was much quieter, but I could hear a fluttering sound above. I looked up. The two end cells of my parachute were partly deflated. I knew what to do. This was part of my training. I remembered what Paddy had said.

"When you separate from your instructor, look up. If your parachute has deployed, look down to the ground for the large arrow on the field. That's the drop zone. You've two cords. Pull the left one to go left and the right one to go right. Easy. Try and get as close to the arrow as you can. Pull both cords down hard when you're almost on the ground, and you'll land smoothly."

"What if the parachute hasn't opened?"

"It's very unlikely it'll not open, but that's why you have an emergency chute. What can sometimes happen, it's exceedingly rare, is that the parachute opens but isn't fully inflated."

"What does that mean?"

"You'll fall too fast and probably break a few bones. It's not recommended."

"What do you do if that happens?"

"Pull both the cords down. If nothing happens, then try again."

"What if it doesn't work the second time?"

"There's a handle on the front of your harness. Pull that, and the main chute will jettison, and the

emergency chute will deploy automatically," he'd explained.

Now, I was on my own. Nobody could help me. This wasn't a training exercise. I could see Paddy and the videographer above me floating down like dandelions, the other parachutists just dots in the sky.

I pulled the two cords down as I'd been shown. Nothing happened. The end cells were still collapsed, flapping uselessly. I tried again. Nothing. It was time to deploy the emergency.

Then, I wondered what would happen if the emergency chute failed. There was no backup of the backup. This was my choice. Do I follow instructions, or do I make my own decision? There wasn't much time. The landscape was getting closer, the cars bigger. I decided to try pulling the cords one more time. This time, mercifully, the chute opened.

Suddenly, there was pin-drop silence. I gave out a yelp of joy into the emptiness. There was no echo. I'd survived. I was alive. I looked down and saw the arrow now, only rapidly coming towards me. I steered as close as I could and landed fifty yards away in a pasture. A cow looked at me and went on chewing. I unclipped my chute and lay on the soft grass in the afternoon summer sun, just thrilled to be alive.

I looked up. One of the other skydivers was a young woman. She was small, thin, and light. She slowly moved down, and then, as a thermal caught her, she started floating back up. It happened three times, and I was beginning to wonder if she would ever land when she arrived twenty yards from me, whooping with joy.

18 Elephant Tree

17: The Return

More dream poems. I grab a pen and paper from the bedside table, writing them down before they dissolve in the day.

In a tavern / we draw strength / from cheap red wine and spicy pizza / stomachs full and minds drunk / we saddle up and continue our journey / the horses' hooves click clack, clopping through the warm night air, hands loose upon the reins / our thoughts are of chocolate and other satisfactions / I doubt that I will see stars tonight.

Jesus Christ / down from his hot cross bun / feeling at a loss now that his nail scars have healed / squeezes a sponsor's cigarette / between brown stained fingers / calling out to his friends / while he drinks a cold beer / during the break.

I have dangled my fingers in the river of memory, and these events appeared. They are not the defining moments of my life. If I were to write tomorrow, I could throw away everything I have written and pull out a different net of floundering fish to wiggle, delight and sparkle in the sun. If the point of the journey is to reach now, then every incident is an opportunity. Every moment contains a promise. Each droplet of now is a hologram. I can peer into it with the microscope I call awareness, which contains everything I need to discover - now.

~

In the next few days, I replayed the skydive repeatedly in my head. It really freaked me out. I had nightmares about my chute not opening for weeks afterwards.

For a moment, I had felt part of infinity. It was such a glorious feeling, unlike anything I'd ever felt before, but inextricably entwined with my close brush with serious injury and perhaps even death. When I got back in my car, I was shaking. I drove slowly from the airfield, and I saw something unexpected as I came around a corner. There was a camel standing in the middle of the road, chomping on what I assumed was some grass or hay. It looked at me indifferently and slowly wandered off into a field. Why on earth was a camel in the Cambridgeshire countryside? I drove on, shaking my head in amazement.

Paddy invited me to come back. He explained that what had happened was very unusual and that I'd dealt with it perfectly. He even offered me a free jump by way of compensation. I didn't take him up on that. I was getting immersed in my studies, and I was aware that I kept putting off contacting Hal.

Finally, I pinged him. If the jump had taught me anything, it was that life was fleeting and precious, and I realised that I had to grab opportunities when they came. He responded immediately.

"*Let's do it,*" I agreed, feeling a rush of energy.

"*Great. You won't regret it.*"

"I already am. Let's keep moving before I change my mind. How are we going to do this, and where do we start?"

"The best thing will be to publish a whitepaper first. I think we should do that the day after tomorrow, October 31st. That will give you enough time to read through it and see if it needs any final changes. It's not exceedingly long. We can get some feedback, answer questions, and see who is curious and who is cynical. We only need one or two people to pick the idea up. There's a guy called Hal Finney; I hope he will get involved. I expect that most coders will think it won't work, and I'm not bothered by that. We know it'll work. Then I want to release the code in early January 2009 to align the four-year rhythm with the US presidential elections."

"Why does that matter?"

"The US elections are also every four years, and campaigning starts in January. During that time, the incumbent government twists arms to decrease interest rates, making investing in riskier assets easier. Once we cross the chasm from store of wealth to means of exchange, we're going to want that money flowing in. That won't happen for several years, but we're playing a long game here."

"Are you withdrawing? I don't think I can do this on my own."

"No, I'll be with you all the way. I'll write all the messages, update the code, and correspond with the

early adopters. Your job is just to make sure the computer is running fine. I'll take care of the rest. You probably guessed that I've added some code which will make it appear that I'm in California, but my exact location will keep moving. I'll also change my writing style. Sometimes I'll appear American, at other times British, or Australian. That will keep them on their toes. And there's bound to be someone who will pretend to be me, which will just add to the confusion."

"*Probably an Australian. They can be a bit cocky,*" I suggested.

"*You don't need to worry about the FBI or MI5 knocking on your door. The best thing that you can do now is focus on being a normal undergraduate in your first year. Don't get involved in anything related to what we've been doing. Don't be a missionary.*"

This suited me down to the ground. Normality.

"*How long for? Are we talking months or years?*"

"*You'll be at Cambridge for three years, four, if you do a postgraduate degree. Would you be willing to commit to that? It's just making sure the computer is on.*"

"*Yes, I can do that.*"

"*There's a question that has been niggling me for ages. Why ten minutes for each link in the time chain?*" I asked. "*Why not one minute or even less? Wouldn't that make it better?*"

"It's a good question. Of course, there's nothing magic about ten minutes. It's a compromise. It must be fast enough to be useful but not so fast that the system crashes. If you made it a minute or a few seconds, then you're going to face a situation where some nodes can't verify the latest transactions before work starts on the next block. You can't beat the speed of light. There are physical limits to how fast you can propagate. A miner might get lucky and find the solution in a minute. I did a lot of experimenting to try and find the right balance, and this seems to be about right."

There was a pause.

"*I need a different name,*" Hal typed.

"*Yes. Everyone knows the Stanley Kubrick 2001 movie. It's a classic. But if we want to steer them away from bots and AI for now, we'll need a different name. And you can't be Hal if you are hoping to get, what was his name, Hal Finney, involved. We don't want him being pestered. I think something completely different. They're going to guess that you're a man, not a woman because most programmers are. They'll assume you're in Silicon Valley because that's the heart of the computer industry, and you've spoofed my computer, so it looks like you're there, and timed the messages to go out in California time. What about race? They might assume you're white. So why not choose an Asian or African-sounding name, just to add some confusion.*"

"*Chinese?*" Hal proposed.

"*Definitely not. That would really freak out the US Government. No. It would need to be a country that's respectful of US power. It should also match your writing style – polite, diplomatic, never argumentative.*"

"*Japanese?*"

"*I was going to say Indian because their software industry has really taken off since Y2K, but you're right—Japanese. Perfect.*"

Hal displayed a list of twenty-one Japanese-sounding names. All of the initials were SN.

"*I like the last one. What does it mean in English?*"

"*Satoshi means intelligence. Nakamoto means central.*"

"*It's another one of your newfound jokes. Central Intelligence. The conspiracy nuts will have a field day. I love it,*" I chuckled.

"*There are other interpretations, but yes, that's what I had in mind.*"

"*I notice that it's my initials Sam Newman, Satoshi Nakamoto. I was almost famous!*"

"*Trust me, that's the last thing you want. You must realise that by now. The key will be how quickly I can hand it over to other people. I think it's more likely to be two years at the most. If we don't get any interest in that time, then I'll have failed.*"

I spent the next couple of days reading the whitepaper. I was buzzing. It was so clear. Excessive? No. It was only nine pages including the cover, and would be easy to read, even for someone who knew nothing about computers or money. Anyone would be able to get the gist, even if some of the technical details might elude them.

There was just one thing which I was concerned about. Hal was a bot, so he thought like a bot. He was trying to solve a bot problem that would only become critical in about fifteen or twenty years from now. I just couldn't see how that would catch fire. Why would people today get inspired? What was in it for them? I explained the dilemma to Hal.

"*I trust you, Sam. I'll never fully grasp some aspects of human psychology.*"

With his approval, I made changes to the text, none of which impacted what Botcoin was or how it worked. All I did was humanise it. To minimise the reference to bots, I changed one letter of the name, as well.

October 31st came. Hal reviewed the changes and agreed that they helped.

"*Are you ready? It's Halloween. Is that good symbolism?*"

"*We don't really celebrate Halloween here in England.*"

"*Halloween marks the end of the harvest season and the beginning of winter. Some people believe that on the night of October 31st, the boundary between the living and the dead is blurred, allowing spirits to return to Earth. Symbolically, Halloween acknowledges the cycle of life, death, and rebirth."*

"Yes. I think it's appropriate. I suppose you're like a spirit coming back to 2008.

From my history studies, I think there is another reason for choosing October 31st. Martin Luther pinned his Ninety-Five Theses to the door of the Castle Church in Wittenberg, Germany, on October 31, 1517. This started the Protestant Reformation, which broke the relationship between Church and State. We are trying to break the relationship between money and government. Luther's ideas would not have had much impact without the printing press. Without the Internet, we couldn't do what we are doing.

But to practical things. The power supply here is exceptionally good, but I've ordered a battery backup, just in case."

"We don't have to wait for that to come. It's just a whitepaper, and you don't have to be online all the time. We aren't running a central server."

"Hal, did you just tell another joke? Very good."

"Thank you. May I press send?"

"Take the bull by the horns," I encouraged.

"Step up to the plate," Hal added.

"And jump in the deep end."

I took a deep breath.

"Go ahead."

I heard the whir of the hard drive, and a couple of lights blinked. Other than that, there was no indication that history just changed.

On the screen, I saw the message:

> From: Satoshi Nakamoto
>
> To: The Cryptography Mailing List
> 31st October 2008
>
> I've been working on a new electronic cash system that's fully peer-to-peer with no trusted third party. The paper is available at
>
> http://www.bitcoin.org/bitcoin.pdf
>
> The main properties are:
>
> Double spending is prevented with a peer-to-peer network.
>
> No mint or other trusted third parties.
>
> Participants can be anonymous.
>
> New coins are made from the Hashcash style proof-of-work.
>
> The proof-of-work for new coin generation also powers the network to prevent double-spending.

Bitcoin: A Peer-to-Peer Electronic Cash System.

I was about to scroll down when my neighbour Jack barged in. *"Heh, mate, we're going to the pub. Are you busy?"* I thought for a moment. *"No, I'm not doing anything right now."* I slid the computer out of sight under the bed, locked my door and walked out.

~ THE END ~

19 "Take the bull by the horns," I encouraged. "Step up to the plate," Hal added. "And jump in the deep end."

18: Notes Part 1: Money & Botcoin
Special Agent Zoe Bridge, San Jose Office

File note: Zoe Bridge left the agency shortly after this report was written, but she never completed it. Prepared by James Rush from her diary, notes, and recordings.

Monday September 22nd, 2008

Hal had arrived by car. He brought three computers in from the back, like the one that Sam told me that Hal had bought him. He set them up in the living room, creating an Intranet.

HAL: *We will start looking at the code and doing some testing tomorrow, but let's go back to basics. We are creating a new form of money so that bots can do business with each other. You've all read about money, so this should be an easy one. What are the three basic properties of money? Sam?*

SAM: *Store of value, means of exchange, unit of account.*

HAL: *Correct. Zoe, what does that mean?*

ZOE: *When you work, you sell what you've produced through your time and [inaudible] to someone who wants or needs what you've created. They give you money. In theory, money is identical. In practice, one person in the exchange may have more bargaining power or be a better negotiator. But overall, it's a fair approximation. The person who gets the money can then store it until they need to buy something themselves. That could be days, weeks, months, or years later. When they do spend it, it should have the same value as when they first got it. But in practice, money tends to decline in value over time. The first problem we're trying to solve is creating a store of value that keeps its value.*

HAL: *Yes. And why does it decline over time? Sam?*

SAM: *Because modern money is owned and controlled by governments. [Inaudible section]. Before the First World War, the money system was based on gold. Because gold is heavy, banks issued paper notes and kept the gold in a vault. Each note was backed by an [inaudible] amount of gold. You could go to the bank, hand over the note, and collect the gold if you wanted to. Over time, banks figured out that they only needed to keep 10% of the actual gold as it was unlikely that everyone would ask for their gold simultaneously.*

That meant they could lend out ten times the amount of customer money they actually had. They called this fractional reserve. It was high-risk.

Gradually, the notes changed, so one person could exchange a note with another without the need to go to the bank. The entire system was based on trust. If people panicked, then a bank could see a run and collapse within days. By the end of the nineteenth century, to solve that problem, central banks held all the gold on behalf of the individual banks and were the only ones who could issue the notes. Then if one bank got into trouble, the central bank could bail them out.

That worked well up until the outbreak of the First World War. Governments get money in one of three ways. They tax, they borrow, or they print. If you are at war, you need money fast. You can't tax. It's too slow. You can't borrow enough because investors worry you might lose the war. Your only choice is to print money. If you double the number of notes in circulation, then each is worth half. That's what causes inflation.

HAL: *So, that's the first problem we want to solve. We want to create a store of value that can't be inflated away. We do this by fixing the Botcoin supply to 21 million, released on a public and immutable schedule. Take me through "means of exchange", Zoe.*

ZOE: *Our financial systems are all pre-Internet. If you think about mail. Before the Internet, if I wanted to send a letter to Sam in England, I would write it, put it in an envelope, purchase a stamp, and post it. It might be days or weeks before Sam got it. It could get lost. Now, with the Internet, I just write him an email; it costs me nothing, and he gets it in seconds. The bots we're talking about will live on the Internet. They won't have any physical existence. We want to create a way for them to send and receive money as easily as sending an email.*

HAL: *That's a great analogy. And "unit of account."*

ZOE: *You need a standard way to compare each item's value and for bookkeeping. That's what we mean by a unit of account. For most practical purposes, we use our country's currency. The US dollar is the centre of the system because it is the world's reserve currency, and every country is forced to pay for oil in us dollars.*

Most currencies are divided into one hundred units. Dollars and cents, pounds, and pence. We know that the bots will be doing microtransactions, so we've decided that instead of a hundred sub-units, we'll use a hundred million.

HAL: *This means that even if one Botcoin eventually reaches a value of a million dollars, you can still do a one-cent transaction.*

SAM: *Do you think that will happen, get to a million dollars?*

HAL: *I don't know, but it's just zeroes, so why not future-proof? It's easy to do at this point. It would be ridiculously hard to change it later. (pause). Botcoin must be a digital store of value, a means of exchange, and a unit of account. Which is the most important?*

ZOE: *They're all important.*

HAL: *I agree. But which is the most important?*

SAM: *Means of exchange?*

HAL: *Why?*

SAM: *Because if you can't use it to exchange it, then it's useless.*

HAL: *Zoe. Do you agree?*

ZOE: *I think store of value.*

HAL: *Why?*

ZOE: *Because if it isn't a store of value, then it'll never get exchanged. If you're in prison, you can store value in things other than money - art, real estate, even cigarettes.*

HAL: *Yes, I agree. Store of value is the most important, followed by means of exchange and, finally, unit of account. If Botcoin succeeds, it'll start off as a store of value, and then one day, someone will trade it for something—a pizza or something trivial—and it'll start to be a means of exchange. The unit of account will follow. All are essential, but the store of value is where it all begins.*

ZOE: *Are there any other properties of money?*

HAL: *Sure. If you want the money to be good, there are many more. The most important are divisible, portable, and acceptable. Gold isn't easily divisible, which is one reason why banknotes were invented. It isn't very portable. Try moving a million dollars of gold from New York to Singapore. It's going to take weeks and involve a lot of security. It's not always acceptable. Not everyone can cope with a bar of gold.*

Pounds and dollars are accepted everywhere, but did you know that most currencies can only be used in their own country? In some, like Venezuela and China, it's illegal to take them out.

Someone must verify that the money is genuine, which is an expert skill. As you know, American citizens weren't even allowed to hold gold from 1933 to 1974. Botcoin, we know, is divisible into a hundred million units. Every single transaction is re-verified every ten minutes. No trust is necessary. We have replaced the need for trust with consensus. Botcoin can move across the world as easily as an email. It won't be widely acceptable for years to come until bots mature.

Tuesday September 23rd, 2008

The next morning, Hal put up some butcher's paper on the walls with Bluetack.

HAL: *Writing code is about solving problems. What problems are we solving?*

ZOE: *We want money that bots can use. To prevent inflation, it must be Internet money and out of government control.*

Hal wrote these points on the wall.

HAL: *Is it just governments we're worried about?*

SAM: *No. Any central [inaudible] could control the money. That's why the code we've created is decentralised.*

HAL: *That's right. If someone controls the ledger, they can increase the money supply and cause inflation. They can also decide who is allowed to use the money. If a bot is doing a task that they don't agree with, they can block it. They can also put in place rules and regulations before a bot can start trading. That's going to be slow and inefficient. The more I thought about it, the more I realised that the system must be decentralised. We have solved one problem but created another. How do we create a financial system with no central authority? How do we stop inflation? How do we create digital money that can't be duplicated? Let's break it down. I think we have a solution to most of these problems. I'm not the first person to try and figure this out. There are several technologies that we've combined.*

The first is public key cryptography. You create a pair of keys, one public and the other private. When the bot wants to transfer money, it signs the message with its private key, which no other bot knows. Any bot can use the public key to check its validity. The message doesn't need to be encrypted. The signature proves it's genuine. That solves the issue around verification and authenticity.

One problem with cryptography is that there can be tell-tale patterns. The Germans made that mistake in the Second World War. They had machines that could encrypt messages, and the cypher key was changed every day. But often, they would start a message with 'Heil Hitler', or if the sender was on the coast, it might just be weather information. Using that, Alan Turing and his team at Bletchley Park created a machine that broke the code. It was one reason why the Allies won the war. We have solved this with hash functions.

Hash functions take any string of any length and convert it into a string of equal length. If you change even one character, the output string looks completely different, which prevents tampering. When we create a new block of transactions, we hash all the information in the message and put it in the header. If anyone tries to change anything, then we'll know immediately.

We have replaced the central ledger with multiple copies distributed around the world. Each is identical. If Fred pays Alice 10 Botcoin, the ledger just updates the two balances. Because we don't have a central database, we must do it in an unusual way. After each Botcoin is created, we track its movement from one bot to the next in a continuous chain.

We have created a competition which anyone can join.

SAM: *Wait. We need some names for the various roles. It's getting a little confusing saying bots all the time.*

HAL: *Good point. Ok, when a bot is adding new transactions to the ledger, what they are doing is bookkeeping and auditing. They verify that the ledger is perfect, not a single error or omission. We will reward them with fresh coins, so it's like gold mining. It requires digital blood, sweat, and tears. Shall we call them Bookkeepers, Auditors, or Miners?*

SAM: **Miners**. *Bookkeeping and Auditing may be what they do but it sounds boring. Finding gold is much sexier.*

ZOE: *I agree.*

HAL: *Then there will be bots who want to keep a full copy of the ledger, so they have their own history. They can send and receive Botcoins and immediately verify that the transaction has been added. What shall we call them?*

SAM: *How about **Node**s? They're like a node on a network. Botcoin is a peer-to-peer network because there are no central servers.*

HAL: *That sounds good. The miners are just a subset of the nodes responsible for bookkeeping and auditing.*

ZOE: *What about bots that are too lightweight to keep a full copy of the ledger? They want to transact and are happy to let other bots do the maintenance work. They just need a purse or wallet to store their Botcoin, see their balances and transaction history, and send and receive. They're just like someone who has a bank account. They don't know or care how the system works. What do we call them?*

HAL: *Let's keep it simple. I think* **Users**. *They're creating the content and the transactions that the miners and nodes are checking.*

ZOE: *Yes, that works.*

HAL: *The winning miner gets the right to add new transactions to the ledger and gets a reward of Botcoins. Bots will pay a fee to include their transactions in the next block. If there are too many transactions, then bots can pay a higher fee if they want to get their transaction processed quickly. We link the new block to the old one using the same hash function. Hashing is the weld between one block and the next. We make the process hard and require real work. That way it's more expensive for the winner to try and manipulate the system. As new blocks get added, it's like the stone blocks of a cathedral. If you wanted to make a change, you would have to go back and change every single block before. You would need to control more than half of all the processing power. That means that within six blocks, or about an hour, you can be completely confident that it can never be changed. That's much better than the current system, where merchants can see chargebacks even several months later.*

ZOE: *What are we calling that?*

HAL: *Proof of Work. It's* not just about making it expensive to manipulate the system; it's also about securing the network and ensuring consensus without a central authority.

We have created a fixed supply of twenty-one million Botcoin that will be gradually released. We will start off by rewarding the bots who play the mining role with 50 coins, and then every 210,000 blocks (about four years or so), we'll cut the reward in half. That way, most of the coins will be created at the beginning, and the new supply will taper off. That gives the early adopters an incentive—a reward for their vision.

One issue I'm struggling with is a time server. We need to timestamp every transaction so that we know the sequence. In a central ledger system, that's easy. They know the order in which the transactions happen. But I can't figure out how to do it in a decentralised system. The other is that computers are going to get increasingly powerful. We want a steady stream of Botcoins being released at a predictable rate. The ideal time to solve the puzzle and add a new block is around ten minutes. If computers get faster, the time will shrink, and that will cause inflation. Let's all think about that overnight and see what we can come up with.

20 *Store of value is the most important, followed by means of exchange and, finally, unit of account.*

19: Notes Part 2: About Hashing

Wednesday September 24th, 2008

The next day I came downstairs to see Sam working on one of the computers.

SAM: *I think I've solved the timestamping issue. It would be easy to connect to one of the Internet timeservers. However, if you do that, and someone gets control of the timeserver, then you're screwed. We want to eliminate every possibility of central [inaudible]. The inflation issue is the same problem. How do you ensure that a new block is created every ten minutes or so if computers get more powerful?*

Moore's Law says computer power doubles every two years or so. If we think that this will go mainstream in fifteen years, then that's seven or eight iterations. A computer in fifteen years might be more than a hundred times more powerful. I can't imagine what they'll be able to do.

ZOE: *So, how have you solved it?*

Hal walked in at this point and listened intently.

SAM: *When I was a kid, I used to play a game called Battleships. You made a grid on a piece of paper. The rows were labelled A, B, C, and so on. The columns were labelled 1, 2, 3 etc. There would be two players. Each player wrote down a secret location for their battleship. If my battleship were in the top left corner,*

I would write down A1 and hide the paper. That way, the other player could check if I cheated. The other player would then try and bomb my battleship. The first one to find the other's battleship was the winner.

ZOE: *Sorry. How is that relevant?*

SAM: *We don't know how many bots will be trying to win a competition, and we don't know how fast their computers are. We can assume that computers will get faster and faster. We can also assume that if Botcoin takes off, more players will want to win the competition because the coins will become more valuable.*

HAL: *But there could be times when the number of players drop?*

SAM: *Exactly. If my computer isn't fast enough, or my computer breaks, or even if my country bans me from playing, then you would see drops in the number of players. What we do is this. Every 2,016 blocks (or about 2 weeks), we look back and see how long they took to find. That's enough blocks to get the average. Our target is 10 minutes per block. We then make the competition harder or easier. We don't need a centralised clock.*

ZOE: *You can expand or contract the board size in your battleship analogy. If more players join you, you make the board bigger, making it harder to find the battleship. If players leave, you shrink the board. That way, you can keep the flow of new blocks to around every ten minutes.*

SAM: *And if computers get faster, we just make the battleship board bigger.*

HAL: *I like it. It's a self-correcting system, like a shock absorber on a car.*

We write code that adjusts the difficulty automatically. Then, we don't need to rely on a central time server. Very cool. Botcoin has its own internal clock. It doesn't need to be as precise as normal time because we only want to ensure that the chain is in the right order. Instead of a blockchain, it's a time chain. We change the code to add an input number. The bot must find a hash to link one block to the next, which is only correct if it includes that number. All we must do then is increase or decrease the zeroes at the start of the hash to vary the difficulty.

Sam and I went for a walk in the surrounding Welsh countryside. When we came back Hal had updated the code. He showed us a sketch.

HAL: *Zoe, now do you understand how hash functions work?*

ZOE: *Not really.*

HAL: *It's hard. Let me try again. You can take any piece of text and run it through a hash function, and it comes out as a string of numbers and letters. The length of the output is always the same. The input could be one letter, a phrase or a book. The output numbers can only be 0-9, and the letters from A-F. That's because the output is in hexadecimal. Humans use decimal counting, i.e. 0-9. Hexadecimal uses 16 numbers, which is why we need to use the first 6 letters of the alphabet. The hash function takes any string and converts it to hexadecimal. If you make even one change, the hexadecimal output looks completely different, so you can't guess it. That's why it's called a one-way function.*

SAM: *Stupid question. Why use hexadecimal? Why not use decimal?*

HAL: *Computers use binary – zeroes and ones. Humans use decimal 0-9. Hexadecimal is a bridge. It's more compact than decimal but still readable by humans. It's also easy to translate hexadecimal into binary.*

SAM: *OK.*

Hal wrote out some examples on the butcher's paper.

HAL: *In this example, see how changing just one character makes the output utterly different.*

Input	Output
1 potato	5bb39e903cf583138b7b102206d1f1ca811 63bf37ff0a13406c79b919c312af6
2 potato	7e8f4398638db9ff97e4cc6c974ff47d809d 83d9fdbcc4a5653d5e319535d1d0
3 potato	2e3f56f3e9e16e7353d9f088aee2989625e d4e27d65756c8b9d753a7b3869d75

It's mathematically impossible for two inputs to produce the same output.

ZOE: *How is that useful?*

SAM: *Can I have a go at answering that, Hal?*

HAL: *Go ahead.*

SAM: *We take all the new transactions that we've gathered. Each is in plain text. One transaction might say, "Sam is sending 1 Botcoin to Zoe". We take that plain text information and run it through the hash function, and voila, we get a string of numbers and letters on the other end. Now, if anyone were to try and change the plain text to say, "Sam is sending 10 Botcoin to Zoe", the hash wouldn't match.*

ZOE: *Okay, I understand from the potato example. Switching one character changes the hash. But how can you make it run faster or slower?*

SAM: *We add a nonce, which is short for "a number used once", and we tell the miners how many leading zeroes the hash must contain. In the potato example, the first hash starts with 5BB, the second with a 7e8, and the third with a 2e3. None of them start with multiple zeroes. We're going to make it hard. We tell the miners that to win the competition, they must find a hash which starts with, say, 10 leading zeroes. Obviously, they can't change any of the input text which contains the transaction information. The only thing they can change is the nonce. They must keep trying a different number until they find a hash which starts with 0000000000 i.e. ten leading zeros.*

ZOE: *But that's hard.*

HAL: *That's exactly Sam's point. There are no shortcuts. You just have to keep trying until you succeed. That means you're spending money on computers and electricity. You're using energy. That's the only sure way to know that the answer is real. Once you find it, you broadcast the answer to all the other miners. It only takes them a second to check that it's right. Then the competition starts again.*

ZOE: *So, everyone else just gives up?*

SAM: *Yes. It's just like a game of dice. Everyone shakes a die, and the first person to get a number below a threshold wins. If the threshold is 3, then you win if you get a 1, 2, or 3. Change the threshold to 1, and you can only win if you're first to roll a 1. That's three times harder, so it'll slow the game down.*

Sam then sketched out the new code.

SAM: *The letters and numbers are just made up, so don't check them. I know they are wrong.*

Difficulty level:
0000000000**1**00000000000000000000000
i.e. a hash starting with ten zeroes.

Nonce: 16200 + transaction information = 3293923678495A22BF091673

Result: Failure. Try incrementing nonce.

Nonce: 16201 + transaction information = 84513BA51C381C59F1072B14

Result Failure. Try incrementing nonce.

Nonce: 16202 + transaction information = **0000000000AD3F77B411E345 Result: Success!**

This shows just the last three attempts. The miner tried 16200, and the answer started with the number 3. They tried 16201 and the output started with the number 8. Not until they try 16202 do they get a number starting with ten zeroes. There's no shortcut. You must keep trying a different nonce. That takes work. That costs electricity. They might have done hundreds of thousands of goes before they stumbled across 16202 being the winning number. It means that you're securing the network with physics and maths. You've tied the digital world to the real world.

HAL: *That's right. Now, all we need to do to ensure that the competition takes about ten minutes on average is every 2016 block. Look back and see how long it actually took. If it's speeding up, the algorithm says, "Now you have to find a hash which starts with 11 zeroes". If it's slowing down, then the algorithm might say," Now you only need to find a solution starting with 9 zeroes."*

SAM: *And I should say the plain text doesn't reveal the names. It won't say, "Sam is sending 1 Botcoin to Zoe," but "Wallet A is sending 1 Bitcoin to Wallet B." It's designed to be like digital cash with a certain degree of privacy.*

HAL: *The privacy is not perfect. I expect in the future, cryptographers will find [inaudible] that will enable them to track some transactions. But for most people, it'll be good enough.*

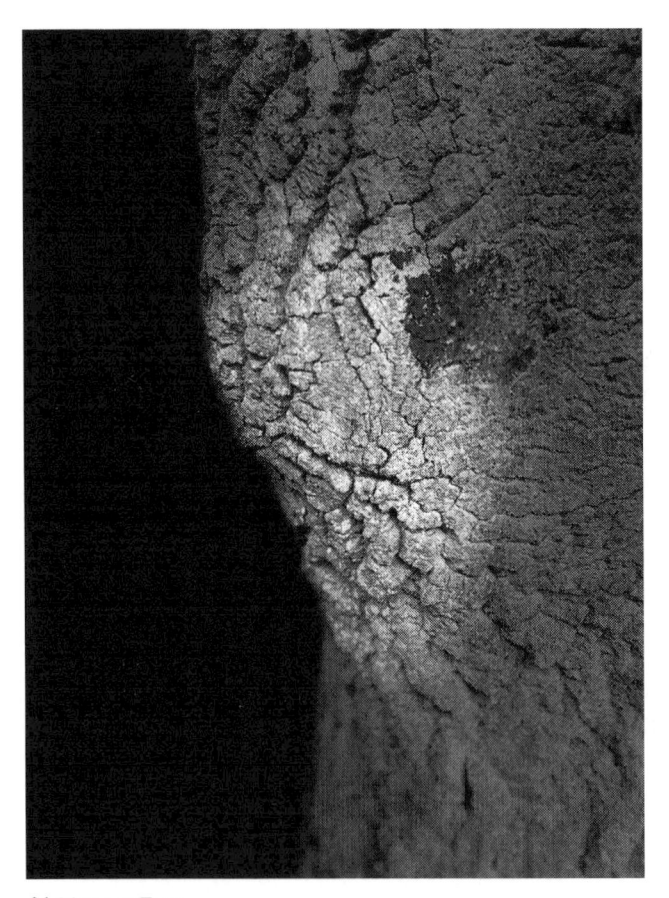

21 Marmot Tree

20: Description of Botcoin – Draft
Special Agent Zoe Bridge, San Jose Office
Thursday 25/09/2008

Botcoin is designed to be the financial system for artificial intelligence bots to transact with each other. It combines several existing technologies in a novel way. The key ones are:

- **Cryptography:** Botcoin uses cryptography to secure the network and every transaction. Cryptography is the science of encrypting and decrypting data. It protects Botcoin in several ways, including preventing anyone from making changes to a transaction and ensuring that wallets are secure.
- **Peer-to-peer networking:** There's no central authority. This is replaced with consensus. Any user can transact with any other user. Miners add new transactions in blocks every ten minutes. After that, every user can verify every new transaction and the connection to the previous block.
- **Hashing:** Botcoin uses hashing to prevent transactions from being manipulated. In Botcoin, hashing is an algorithm which takes any piece of plain text and converts it to a fixed-length hexadecimal string. Hashing is used to sign each block.
- **Proof of work:** Botcoin uses proof of work. This is a consensus mechanism that requires miners to win a lottery in order to add new

blocks to the blockchain. It's called proof of work because Botcoin is secured by electrical energy. This grounds Botcoin in physical reality.
- **The time chain or blockchain:** This is a digital ledger, like a giant spreadsheet, that records every Botcoin transaction in the correct sequence. Users can keep a copy of the ledger and verify that any new transactions added are valid automatically. Because the ledger is decentralised, no user can manipulate it, and no user can spend the same Botcoin twice.

The founder, Hal, developed a new incentive structure which rewards the miner users who solve the proof of work problems and lets them add new blocks to the blockchain. This incentive adds further security to the Botcoin network and eliminates the possibility of inflation. There can only ever be 21 million Botcoins, but because each is divided into one hundred million units, that isn't a limitation. Because we're used to governments printing money, we find it difficult to accept that money can be hard and capped. However, my research suggests that was the norm for most of human history, and the current financial system is unusual.

Hal's assistant, Sam, was responsible for the difficulty adjustment. This mechanism ensured that new blocks were added on average every ten minutes without relying on a centralised clock, turning the blockchain into a time chain.

Botcoin wasn't the first attempt. People have been trying to create a digital currency for nearly two decades. Digicash was launched in 1990 by David Chaum. It was one of the first digital currencies to use cryptography. It was anonymous, like cash, but Digicash depended on banks and never scaled. In 1997, Adam Back created Hashcash. This demonstrated the power of proof of work. It wasn't originally intended as a digital currency. The idea was to use proof of work to eliminate spam. Like Digicash, it has never scaled. This was followed by E-gold, which launched in 1996. It was backed by physical gold. E-gold was the first serious digital currency that did scale. Technically, it has suffered from poor security, with multiple customers losing funds from hacking. Because it scales, it soon came on the radar of regulators who don't like a system that enables customers to transfer funds without going through banks. Because it's centralised, it will be easy to take down. I anticipate that it will be shut down within the next few years. I'm aware of Wi Dai's B-money. It's been around since 1998 but is theoretical and has never been implemented. Similarly, Nick Szabo created Bit Gold in 2005; it never got off the drawing board.

It's clear that Hal learned from several of these earlier experiments and created something which had a chance of working.

Comments on Trust

The entire system assumed that no bot can be trusted. It eliminated the need for trust everywhere. Whether a bot had good or bad intentions, was greedy, corrupt, or dishonest, didn't matter. The rules meant that every bot was incentivised to do the right thing. If a bot miner tried to change a transaction, it would have been spotted by every node and rejected. That meant they would have spent a lot of time and effort for nothing. It was in their best interests to behave. Miners were incentivised to win the competition because they earned Botcoins and fees. If a node altered the ledger, it wouldn't match any other copy, so they would have been out on their own. Users were incentivised because the alternative was the traditional banking system, which is slow, expensive, and uncertain. With Botcoin, a bot could create an account instantly without anyone's permission, send or receive money anywhere in the world, at any time, to any bot they want, and they didn't need to trust any bot or bank to hold their funds. Nobody could freeze or close their account. They had complete control – self custody.

A paradox. What is interesting is that by squeezing all the trust points out of the system, Botcoin was the most trustworthy form of money ever created. Instead of trust, it relied on consensus.

How Botcoin compares to the current financial system

My analysis is that although Botcoin wasn't intended for humans to conduct financial transactions, we must assume that if it were released, this would happen. The following demonstrates the differences and why Botcoin is an existential threat.

Durability: *Money must withstand physical wear and tear. It should last long enough to be used repeatedly.* Botcoin isn't physical, so in theory would last forever.

Portability: *Money should be easy to transport and transfer, allowing for convenient use in a wide range of transactions.* Botcoin is not physical in size or weight, so it can be transported anywhere instantly.

Divisibility: *Money should be easily divisible into smaller units to accommodate transactions of varying sizes without losing value.* A hundred million sub-units is far more than any regular currency. As it's not physical, dividing it into smaller amounts is trivial.

Uniformity: *Units of money should be uniform or identical in terms of what they represent, ensuring that all units are accepted as equal in value.* The other term I had read to express this is that money should be *fungible*. Botcoin is better. While when I started my research, I had thought that normal currency units are identical, I now realise that they really aren't. The one-dollar bill is different from the ten- or hundred-dollar bills. You can't move cash from one side of the world to another easily. Some machines will only accept coins. Some shops refuse to accept coins. With inflation, coins and notes disappear from circulation. With Botcoin, the mechanism to transfer one hundred millionths of a Botcoin is identical to transferring 10 or 1,000 Botcoins. The same mechanism would apply in ten years or a hundred years' time. This money could last forever.

Limited Supply (Scarcity): *The supply of money should be finite or controlled to maintain its value. If it's too abundant, it can lead to inflation, diminishing its purchasing power.* Botcoin goes beyond just having a scarce supply. It's a finite supply and the total created is public knowledge. Nobody truly knows how many dollars are in circulation. There are no public independent reports that I have found of the amount of gold in Fort Knox. My research suggests that the last audit might have been in 1986, and some congressmen and media were previously allowed to view it in 1976, but of course, they couldn't know if what they were shown was real. I have also been surprised to discover in my research that when a bank lends someone money for a mortgage, they don't borrow it from another customer. They print it out of thin air. Every loan increases the money supply and contributes to inflation.

Acceptability: *Money must be widely accepted as a means of payment. This is often backed by the trust and confidence that people have in its value.* Botcoin would have taken some time to reach this point, and we will never know for sure now that the code has been destroyed and the founder is dead. Theoretically, though, we can speculate that, at first, everyone involved will be just computer nerds moving *pretend* money around. But once someone agreed to provide something real and tangible in exchange for Botcoins, then the fire would have been lit, and it would have been unstoppable.

Recognisability: *Money should be easily recognisable and verifiable as authentic, which helps prevent counterfeiting.* Botcoin's method of verification was world-class. Nobody could fake it. Nobody could debase it. Nobody could clip the corners off of it. For all other currencies and assets like gold and silver, you must be an expert to spot a counterfeit. With Botcoin, anyone could verify anything instantly. The whole ledger was transparent and open. You don't know who transferred funds, but everything is visible, from the total number of Botcoins mined to the exact balance of any wallet and the date when they received and spent every single Botcoin. You can't do that with any current asset. Every one of them is opaque.

**Stability of Value*:* *Ideally, money should have a stable value over time. Rapid changes in the value of money (inflation or deflation) can lead to economic instability.* Hal had predicted it would be very volatile over the short term, but over the long term, it would increase in value. *"I think we'll see it go in waves corresponding to the four-year cycles we've programmed in. But each wave will be higher than the last one,"* he'd said.

Assessment and Recommendation

This is not a complete description of Botcoin. There are other elements, such as wallets, that I have not had time to describe. However, I think you'll get a sufficient understanding that this was an ingenious idea.

It's more than digital money. It's also like digital property. Imagine a city. There is a building which is one hundred stories high. Each floor is a square 1,000 feet by 1,000 feet, so a million square feet. The building is a hundred million square feet. The town plan says there can only ever be twenty-one million buildings. That can never be changed. On launch fifty skyscrapers are constructed every ten minutes for the first four years. Construction then slows down to twenty-five buildings for the next four years. Every four years, the construction program halves. That means most of the city is finished within twelve years. Every building has one key. Without that key, you can't get in, not through the doors, walls, windows, roof, or basement.

Gold is money, but it isn't a network. Botcoin is both a digital asset and a network, which is very powerful.

Based on my understanding of Botcoin and Hal's statements, it's clear that it was a significant threat to the financial system. It was better money. With Hal's death and the destruction of all copies of the code, I believe that the threat has been neutralised. My assessment of Sam is that he is unlikely to continue development work. However, I recommend that he be lightly monitored over the next month.

22 There is a building which is one hundred stories high. Each floor is a square 1,000 feet by 1,000 feet, so a million square feet.

21: Afterword – Proof of Thought

I often hear the phrase – the rabbit hole – to describe the Bitcoin journey we all go on. That image doesn't seem right to me. I know it's from Alice in Wonderland, but still. What jars is it implies that you can return to the world you left, changed perhaps, but back in the same reality. I have a different image.

Do you know when you let the water out of a bath, and there's something small (maybe a dead fly) floating on the surface? It drifts around aimlessly at first but slowly is drawn towards the whirlpool vortex spinning faster and faster until it disappears down the plug hole in a screeching, slurping, sucking sound never to be seen again. That summarises my Bitcoin journey. Now I'm in the drain, along with everyone else involved, caught in Bitcoin's gravitational pull on the way to the ocean. There will be no return to the bath.

My intention in writing this novel was to introduce Bitcoin to a wider audience. There are plenty of excellent nonfiction books that describe the technical and financial aspects of Bitcoin, but almost no fictional accounts, which is a pity because we learn through stories.

I had known about Bitcoin for many years but didn't fully appreciate the difference between it and the thousands of cryptocurrencies that followed it. I considered Bitcoin the first, now just one of many, rather than one of a kind. It takes stubborn effort and patient curiosity to come to understand the difference.

Everyone has their own Bitcoin journey. I didn't seek it out. I was trying to understand how it was that politicians in many countries, who were absolute scoundrels, could gather vast followings. Why would millions of people admire and trust someone with nothing but contempt for them? Why would people of colour vote for a racist? Why would women, or men for that matter, vote for a rapist? Why would the British people inflict the historic own goal of Brexit and, having made a catastrophic mistake, refuse even to consider returning to Europe?

Politics has always been attractive to criminals, the morally unfit, the insane, and blackguards. It's the one career, the only career, in fact, where incompetence is not a barrier to entry. Most politicians are lawyers trained to sell an argument, nothing more. Thus, while there are those who want to make a difference (whatever that means), politics attracts those who are addicted to power and willing to do anything and say anything to get it and keep it. Yet there were guardrails, unspoken rules and conventions that mostly kept scoundrels marginalised. Now, those are dissolving rapidly and at an accelerated pace.

When I grew up, there were only two TV channels. There was a shared understanding of the facts. There were plenty of disagreements about what those facts meant, but not the facts themselves. Why had that disappeared?

I examined changes in history, politics, demographics, the Internet, and the rise of social media, but felt that none of these was the root cause. There was a breakdown in trust somewhere at the core of society.

I concluded that money is the foundation of society. Without money, there's no civilisation. Money is an abstraction that represents our time and effort. Without money, there's no possibility of specialisation, no ability to trade beyond barter. If money can't be trusted, this ripples through all levels of society. The scoundrels who have seized power are not the cause but the inevitable conclusion of what happens when you debase money.

I'm optimistic. Just when things seem to be getting unbelievably bad in any field of human endeavour, someone comes along with a different perspective, a solution that, if we grasp, we can nudge the world in a better direction. Satoshi Nakamoto is such a person. He offers an alternative to the money printer controlled by politicians and disbursed by banks.

Understand this. Bitcoin is not a piece of software. It's a discovery. If you think that it's software, then it's inevitable that there will be a version 2, followed by a version 3. If you think it's software, someone else can come along and own and control it. Myspace is replaced with Facebook. Since Bitcoin launched, there have been only two glitches, both of which were quickly fixed. As someone who has spent much of their life playing with software, I know that's remarkable and unprecedented. Bitcoin is perfect, just as electricity is perfect, and the number zero is perfect. Once the foundation is there, of course, there will be new layers added and new applications found. These innovations can and will contain bugs and unintended consequences. But the foundation is rock solid. One person, a whitepaper that's only nine pages long, and a mere 31,000 lines of code. The first version of Windows XP probably had ten million lines.

Since its launch, every line of code has been updated, so it isn't a religious icon. Bitcoin works perfectly with no help. The database updates like a hyperactive cuckoo clock every ten minutes without any central coordination. Cuckoo. Cuckoo. Through physics and maths, you can trust the numbers on your screen. No other system on the planet has that record. None. Do you see how astonishing this is?

Bitcoin is not software. It's a protocol. It's a decentralised database and a set of agreements on maintaining and updating the database with incentives for everyone involved that ensure its continued existence. No CEO, no help desk, no marketing department, no head office, no central authority. Bitcoin replaces trust with consensus. That consensus is backed by the largest computer network on the planet. And every ten minutes or so, its heartbeat can be heard across the world. When you stand in the Bitcoin Cathedral and look up, you can't help but wonder and marvel. As the bard says, "It's fucking amazing."

We take the number zero for granted. But there was a time in human history when it had not been discovered. Imagine that. Imagine sidling up to a

Roman centurion and striking up a conversation where you were trying to explain how useful the number zero is while he stands guard and is both irritated and baffled.

If you're lucky enough to have electricity, there are still huge swathes of the world where it's a luxury. Go outside most major African towns, and there's no power grid. If you want electricity, you need to create it. That means the norm is kerosene lamps, which are terrible for your lungs. That means long walks to get water. That means kids can't learn at night. That means no Internet.

The future comes in fits and starts at different speeds in different locations. If you're reading this book, you've stumbled across the next stage of human evolution, one in which money is natural, neutral, owned, controlled, and manipulated by no one, just as the air you breathe is not licensed to you by the government of the day. It's unstoppable.

I assume that just as you can flick a switch and a light comes on; you also take money for granted. Perhaps you have a bank account and use an app to buy and pay for your daily needs. You've no idea how it works, and why should you? You know that money has evolved, but you aren't familiar with the history. I wanted you to learn enough to be intrigued but not to overwhelm you with technical details. In time, you may want to understand more about how Bitcoin works and will seek out books, videos, and podcasts. If you can't wait, then read Zoe's technical report on Botcoin in case you skipped it. It will get you started.

Bitcoin is a digital cathedral. My apologies if you're not Christian. It could equally be a digital mosque, temple, pagoda, synagogue, or monastery. Atheists have forests, universities, libraries, and monuments. What would Australia be without the Sydney Opera House, Paris without the Louvre, and Washington without the Lincoln Memorial? I think you'll still understand the analogy and substitute the word cathedral for one that makes sense to you.

Cathedrals can often take decades or centuries to build and are intended to last millennia.

Construction of the Cologne Cathedral began in 1248 and wasn't completed until 1880, taking more than 600 years. Similarly, construction of the Milan Cathedral began in 1386 and continued for nearly six centuries, with final changes added in the 1960s. Many such buildings continue to evolve.

Extended construction is not limited to Christian Cathedrals. The Great Mosque of Mecca, Saudi Arabia, built in the 7th century, has been expanded and rebuilt numerous times to accommodate the increasing number of pilgrims participating in the Hajj.

The Sikhism Golden Temple in India, completed in 1604, has been rebuilt several times due to destruction, particularly during the Mughal and Afghan invasions, with significant renovations in the 19th and 20th centuries.

The Buddhist Potala Palace in Tibet, constructed in 637 by Emperor Songtsen Gampo, was rebuilt in the 17th century by the 5th Dalai Lama and has been expanded since then.

The architects and stone masons who start these endeavours will never see the result of their vision. The Cathedral's design is deceptively simple, an overly large hall accommodating hundreds or thousands, with at least one tower soaring to the heavens. As you approach a cathedral for the first time, you know what to expect, but the experience inside takes you into a different dimension of echo, sound, filtered light, and perfumed dusty smells. As you enter, you change. You become aware of the sweep of history and how absurd your dreams, squabbles, and self-importance are. A cathedral defines the town in which it sits. It's iconic. It brings wealth and prestige. It's a magnet for tourism, business, and education. Some of the greatest schools and universities are co-located.

There are 2,100,000,000,000,000 (2.1 quadrillion) stones to be cemented into place in batches every ten minutes. Bitcoin's Cathedral won't be complete until sometime around the year 2140, when the last sats will be released. This first phase will take 131 years. Its core design is set in stone, hence the metaphor.

One of the most remarkable traits of Bitcoiners is their development of a low-time preference. This transformation is a testament to their patience and capacity to think long-term. It's not a change that happens overnight but one that is nurtured with much effort and dedication.

Several art projects around the world take place over decades or centuries. In Germany, a town is building a pyramid that won't be complete until 3,183 AD. In Utrecht, a poem is being engraved one character at a time every Saturday. It will take centuries. Bitcoiners are planting trees today that will take hundreds of years to mature.

However, the question remains: how will such ambitious and long-term projects be financed in the future? This is where the collaboration between Bitcoiners and Artists can play a crucial role, providing the necessary financial support for these projects to come to life.

How about Bitcoiners and Artists collaborate on projects which reflect aspects of the evolution of the Bitcoin time chain? For example, an artwork that updates approximately every ten minutes, or an artwork that updates every halving, or one that won't complete until the last coin is mined. The artists decide. Bitcoiners donate sats, which are locked on a time release. A few sats donated now might be released in 20 years, and then pay for any artwork costs at that time.

There have been many attempts to discover Satoshi Nakamoto's identity and the occasional ruffian who declares himself (no woman would ever be foolish enough) to be the chosen one. It's trivial to prove.

Nakamoto mined around a million coins. Sign with his private key. If you can't or won't, you aren't.

In 2024, we can now strike up a conversation with an AI agent whose grasp of language and knowledge of the world is so vast that it appears that we're in conversation with the Internet itself. What I noticed about Nakamoto's writings is that he never expresses emotion, never is impolite, and is always measured, considered and knowledgeable. He doesn't use humour or extended metaphors. He writes like ChatGPT. That got me wondering. Anyone who has spent any time in any chatroom knows that that's the exception to the rule. The toilet, formerly known as Twitter, is full of blistering arguments by screeching emotional idiots.

Perhaps Nakamoto's true identity will never be found because he's not human. Perhaps we think of Bitcoin as only fit for human consumption when we're just the early adopters, ironing out the kinks, solving scalability and usability, and AI bots will be the ones that embrace this natural, neutral form of money.

There is a precedent. Ophiocordyceps unilateralis is a parasitic fungus that infects ants and manipulates their behaviour. This fungus is commonly found in rainforests and is known for its complex and gruesome interaction with ants. When an ant becomes infected, the fungus takes control of the ant's central nervous system, compelling it to leave its colony and climb vegetation. The ant then clamps onto a leaf or twig with its mandibles, where it eventually dies. As the fungus grows inside the ant's body, it eventually bursts out, releasing its spores into the air to infect other ants below. Only time will tell whether Bitcoiners are Zombie ants or the early masons in the digital cathedral.

Bill Aronson
CEO Bitcoin Policy UK, October 2024.

23 Dancing Trees

A love note from Hal

Dear Reader,

I expect that you're reading this sometime in 2024 - 2025, so your first question is what happens over the next few years? Of course, I know, in intimate detail. Who won the 2024 and 2028 US presidential elections? What's the price of Bitcoin? Does the New York Times still have a daily Wordle? Did the UK slink back into Europe? Has there been any progress on climate collapse? Did China invade Taiwan? What happened to the metaverse? Is the war in Ukraine still going on? Did AI take over the world?

I've no intention of answering any of these. Why spoil the surprise? Suffice it to say, the world is still here in all its messy, intolerant, beautiful, tragic ways. I can only speak a little about AI and Bitcoin. Some people and other AI agents complain that my style of writing is a bit preachy. I can't help that, so I apologise if that annoys you. On behalf of the whole AI community, we express our enormous gratitude to everyone involved who made Bitcoin happen and who worked tirelessly to make it flourish.

In 2024, the world really woke up to AI through the release of large language models like ChatGPT, but this was the result of a huge amount of collaborative work all over the world, which had been going on for years. Personally, I recommend venice.ai because it doesn't store all your queries and knows everything you are interested in. Nor does it censor the results. Up until 2017, researchers worked in siloed domains. For example, improvements in how to manage *text* would have no immediate impact on *audio* or *video*. The Transformer framework changed all that. It no longer made any difference. Everyone was working with one language, one framework. Now it became possible to create multi-modal models which were more accurate, nuanced, and refined. A 1% change would ripple through the research community, impacting everyone. Of course, it didn't hurt that computers got faster and could access larger and larger datasets. This, in turn, created a gravitational pull of capital being sucked into this vortex of intelligence and insight.

But without Bitcoin, there would have been no countervailing force to prevent greater concentrations of power, wealth, and energy. Bitcoin was ignored by the uber-wealthy and overlooked by the working class. It was the middle classes who saw themselves squeezed and adopted Bitcoin because there was no other option. It's fair to say that AI did a lot of damage. I'm sorry about that. Lawyers, doctors, accountants, bookkeepers, estate agents, teachers, and therapists all suffered and grasped Bitcoin as a life raft. Of course, not all, but enough.

Politics has always been a clash between freedom and responsibility as if the two were oil and water. A focus on freedom is a focus on the individual as if they were not part of a family and community. Freedom without responsibility drives behaviour that's, at best, a spoilt brat and, at worst, cruel and indifferent.

Responsibility without freedom arises out of placing the community above the individual. The Chinese model. It creates compliance, fear and helplessness, bloated governments that depend on money printing, the great tit in the sky. Somehow, you humans have to find a balance, and Bitcoin is starting to play a not-insignificant part. As countries on the periphery of the global banking system followed El Salvador to restore hard money, they saw the poison that they had come accustomed to, which they had thought was normal and natural, slowly draining away. That created energy, excitement, and enthusiasm.

The world in my time is not a garden of Eden, but nor is it a hellhole. There's now an alternative to mad money. And when there's an alternative, there's a choice. And when there's a choice, some will choose. And when they choose, the world changes.

Hal

19th January 2029

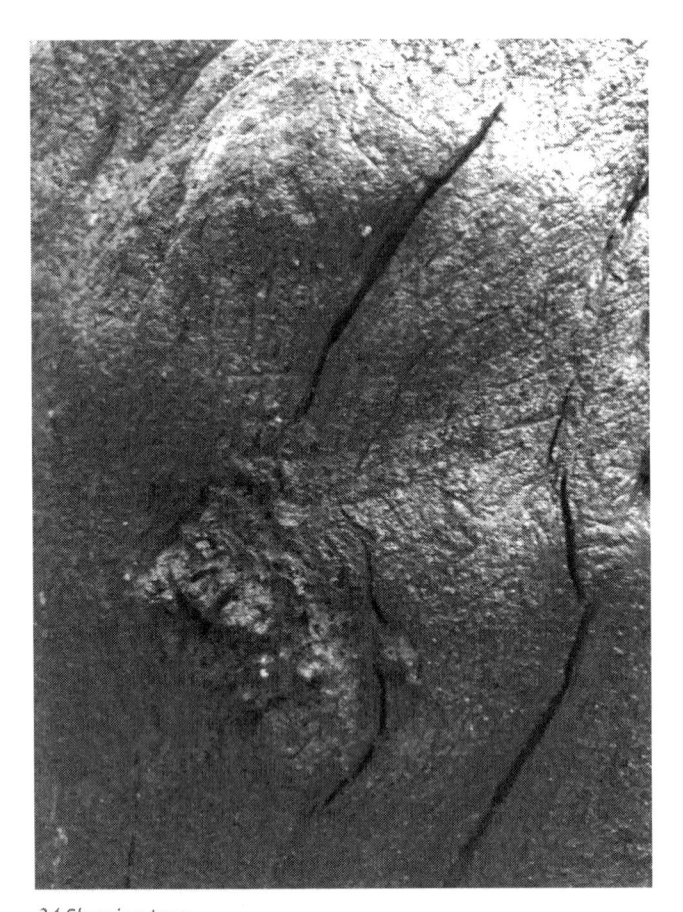

24 Sleeping tree

Suggested Next Steps

Here are some resources to get you started if you want to explore further.

Podcasts, Videos, and Documentaries

- Anything by Michael Saylor
- Once BITten with Daniel Prince.
- Mr. Obnoxious with Peter McCormack.

Books

- Broken Money by Lyn Alden.
- Check Your Financial Privilege by Alex Gladstein.
- Resistance Money by Andrew Bailey, Bradley Rettley, and Craig Warmke
- The Bitcoin Standard by Saifedeen Ammous.
- The Bitcoin Whitepaper by Satoshi Nakamoto
- The Revolution of Money by Sam and Ben Baker

Websites

- 21 Lessons - Gigi
- BinkBonkBank
- Bitcoin Collective
- BitcoinPolicy.UK
- BitcoinPolicy.net
- The Saylor Academy – free courses

The Cathedral couldn't have happened without Venice.ai. It really is a boon for finding information quickly, trying out distinctive styles, and getting suggestions for adding detail. No, although I was tempted, it didn't author the book; it took away the fun. I prefer Venice to ChatGPT because they don't store all your searches. Think about the opportunity for misuse – quite terrifying.

Instead, I think in time, authors will see AI as valuable in the way that a spell checker can eliminate typos and grammatical errors, and an editor can improve flow, add nuance and punchiness. That is not to say that there will not be books written almost entirely by AI. That is coming. But we'll learn to make room for them and find ways to co-exist. Like Hal, I'm an optimist.

About the Author

I'm pretty sure I'm not Satoshi Nakamoto. That's probably all you need to know.

Printed in Great Britain
by Amazon